Inhalants

Myra Weatherly

—The Drug Library—

Enslow Publishers, Inc.
44 Fadem Road   PO Box 38
Box 699   Aldershot
Springfield, NJ 07081   Hants GU12 6BP
USA   UK

Copyright © 1996 by Myra Weatherly

All rights reserved.

No part of this book may be reproduced by any means without the written permission of the publisher.

Library of Congress Cataloging-in-Publication Data

Weatherly, Myra.
　　Inhalants / Myra Weatherly.
　　　　p. cm.—(The Drug library)
　　Includes bibliographical references and index.
　　Summary: Discusses some of the chemical substances which people inhale for a quick high, the dangers of "huffing," the toxic effects of such substances, and social aspects of inhalant abuse.
　　ISBN 0-89490-744-1 (alk. paper)
　　1. Solvent abuse—Juvenile literature. [1. Solvent abuse. 2. Substance abuse.]
　　I. Title. II. Series.
　　RC568.S64W43　1996
　　362.29—dc20　　　　　　　　　　　　　　　　　　　　　　　　95-42818
　　　　　　　　　　　　　　　　　　　　　　　　　　　　　　　　　　CIP
　　　　　　　　　　　　　　　　　　　　　　　　　　　　　　　　　　AC

Printed in the United States of America

10 9 8 7 6 5 4 3 2 1

Photo Credits: Library of Congress, pp. 8, 10, 12; Sara Turner, pp. 19, 22, 27, 34, 37, 40, 51, 66, 71, 87; Texas Prevention Partnership, pp. 62, 84.

Cover Photo: Sara Turner

Contents

1 The History of Inhalant Abuse 5

2 Poisonous Effects of Solvents 16

3 The Dangers of Aerosols 30

4 Amyl Nitrite, Butyl Nitrite,
and Nitrous Oxide 45

5 Social Aspects of Inhalant Abuse ... 56

6 Personal Aspects
of Inhalant Abuse 69

7 Treatment and Prevention 80

Where to Go for Help 93

Chapter Notes 95

Glossary 106

Further Reading 109

Index 111

1
The History of Inhalant Abuse

In Fox Lake, Illinois, fourteen-year-old Randy Plasky sniffed Scotch Guard™ fabric spray with his friends in an empty lot. After a few sniffs, Randy lost consciousness and died.[1]

Nathan Wilson died in the men's room of a Cincinnati, Ohio, theater. A container of butane cigarette-lighter fluid and a plastic bag were nearby. In his pockets were several bottles of typewriter correction fluid. Nathan was eleven years old.[2]

The parents of sixteen-year-old Thane Trimm found him dead in the family garage in Bangor, Maine. He had inhaled gasoline fumes from his all-terrain vehicle.[3]

Carla Hinkle, sixteen, was buried in her "Lady Canes" softball uniform in St. Petersburg, Florida. The teenager's death resulted from inhaling butane.[4]

Inhalants

Do you know what these young people had in common? They experimented with inhaling—or what is known on the street as "huffing"—the fumes from chemical substances found in ordinary household products. They used these materials, which are called inhalants, for a quick high. Huffing carries a high price! These young people paid with their lives.

Inhalant abuse is a growing problem worldwide, but it is not a new phenomenon. The act of breathing in chemicals to change states of consciousness is thousands of years old.

Ancient Times

Inhaling substances for their intoxicating effects has a long history. The practice of inhalation can be traced to the ancient Greeks. At Delphi in the ancient Greek world, a priestess would inhale carbon dioxide produced by burning laurel leaves.[5] This brought on an ecstatic, mind-altering experience. In this altered state, the priestess would give predictions that were interpreted and used by all who gathered around her.

Perfumes and ointments were widely used in ancient Egypt and biblical Palestine as part of religious worship. Archaeologists, scientists who study the people, customs, and life of ancient cultures, have discovered stone altars from the ancient cities of Babylon and Palestine that were used to burn incense made of aromatic spices and woods. In most cases, during these seemingly innocent practices, psychoactive drugs were being inhaled.

In the Mediterranean islands twenty-five hundred years ago and in Africa hundreds of years ago, smoke was inhaled from burning marijuana leaves. Native Americans in North and South America inhaled hallucinogenic substances during some of their religious observances.[6]

Inhalant Abuse in the Eighteenth and Nineteenth Centuries

Many instances of drug abuse stemmed from legitimate treatment for a medical problem. As more volatile agents, substances that could easily be turned into vapor or gas, were produced, inhaling these substances produced intense effects. In the eighteenth and nineteenth centuries, nitrous oxide, ether, and chloroform were commonly abused drugs in North America, Great Britain, and parts of Europe.[7]

Nitrous Oxide

Discovered in 1776 by Sir Joseph Priestley, nitrous oxide (N^2O) was first mixed that same year by Sir Humphry Davy. Davy learned that inhaling the gas resulted in feelings of excitement accompanied by uncontrollable fits of laughter. Nitrous oxide became known as the "laughing gas." Poets Samuel Coleridge and Robert Southey, and the British physician and scholar Peter Roget (author of *Roget's Thesaurus*) attended Davy's N^2O parties.[8] In 1799, after observing the reduction of pain under the influence of nitrous oxide, Davy suggested that it be used during surgery. It would be another forty-five years before testing for this possibility began.

Records show that American students used nitrous oxide for recreational purposes in the early nineteenth century. One student quit medical school and went into the nitrous-oxide business, giving demonstrations and selling the inhalant for twenty-five cents per dose. Attending one of these demonstrations was dentist Horace Wells. The following day, Wells "inhaled some nitrous oxide and felt no discomfort when the student

American dentist Horace Wells (1815–1848) conducted public demonstrations showing the effects of inhaling "laughing gas"—nitrous oxide.

entrepreneur pulled one of his teeth—an experience Wells realized would forever change dentistry."[9] Dentists today still use nitrous oxide for many procedures.

Ether

The abuse of ether—ether drinking and ether sniffing—occurred at least as early as the 1790s.

The major nineteenth century outbreak of ether sniffing occurred in Ireland. When the British government placed a large tax on alcoholic beverages, ether, which was not taxed, was distilled in London and shipped to Draperstown and other places in Northern Ireland by the ton. Ether was preferred by many to whiskey, which was expensive. Ether left no hangover, and if a user was arrested for drunkenness, he or she would be sober by the time he or she reached the police station. A surgeon visiting Draperstown, Ireland, in 1878 described the main street as smelling like his surgery room, where he used ether as an anesthetic. By 1890, government regulations limiting the sale of ether were imposed.

Ether inhalation as a substitute for alcohol was widespread among the upper classes in England during the late nineteenth century. Abusers were also reported in France, Russia, and Norway.

There were reports of ether drinking and ether sniffing by students at universities in both England and the United States during the nineteenth century. At least one professor, by his own account, engaged in the recreational use of ether. Dr. Oliver Wendell Holmes of the Harvard Medical School "inhaled ether at a time when it was popularly supposed to produce mystical or 'mind-expanding' experiences."[10]

Dr. Oliver Wendell Holmes (1809–1894), author and professor at Harvard Medical School, inhaled ether for its "mind-expanding" effects.

Chloroform

Chloroform was discovered in Germany, France, and the United States in 1831. Accounts of chloroform abuse in the United States were reported that same year. Chloroform, which takes a liquid form at room temperatures, gives off vapors which are very powerful when inhaled. Dentist Horace Wells was the first person in the United States to use nitrous oxide in surgery. He died in 1849 of chronic chloroform abuse.[11]

In Scotland in 1847, Dr. James Y. Simpson, an early anesthesiologist, introduced chloroform as an aid during surgery and childbirth. There was religious opposition to its use. Simpson referred to Genesis 2:21 in the Bible to show that God used anesthesia before removing Adam's rib to create Eve: "So the Lord God caused a deep sleep to fall upon the man, and while he slept took one of his ribs . . ." The controversy died down, and the anesthetic use of chloroform became so popular that Queen Victoria (1819–1901) knighted Simpson after he used chloroform to deaden her pain during the delivery of her eighth child. The practice gradually fell out of favor, due to other anesthetics becoming more popular.[12]

Inhalant Abuse in the Twentieth Century

"The twentieth century brought on the use of gasoline and many other volatile compounds. . . . The present period of use of inhalants [as a source of drug abuse] probably dates from the 1920s but expanded rapidly following World War II."[13]

Incidents of inhalant abuse were reported between the mid-1800s and the mid-1900s. Most of these cases grew out of

Queen Victoria (1819–1901) conferred the order of knighthood upon Dr. James Simpson after he used chloroform to deaden the pain during the delivery of her eighth child.

legitimate treatment for medical problems. One case involved a man whose doctor prescribed an anesthetic to treat a facial twitch. After the treatment was no longer needed, the man continued to take the drug for its mind-altering effects.[14]

Nonmedical use of inhalants has been reported in many parts of the world. Sweden published reports of sniffing behavior in 1948. Another early account describes an outbreak of gasoline sniffing in Warren, Pennsylvania, in 1951.[15] Inhalant abuse by large populations was not reported in scientific literature until the early 1950s. During the 1950s and 1960s, numerous articles appeared in magazines and newspapers describing young people sniffing glue.

During the 1960s, other types of inhalants, such as solvents that dissolve other substances and aerosol cans of products that can be sniffed, became popular and continue to be used. One of the most popular inhalants continues to be the gas nitrous oxide. Tighter restrictions have decreased its availability. More recently, amyl nitrite and butyl nitrite—substances that stimulate the heart—have increased in popularity.

Research studies show the use of inhalants—which has been rising in the United States since the early 1980s—is highest during early adolescence. A 1994 survey revealed that 25 percent of eighth graders acknowledged use of illicit drugs at least once during their lifetimes, an increase from the previous year. The national figures rose to 35 percent when inhalants were included.[16] Researchers attribute this increase to lack of awareness of the dangers of drugs, particularly inhalants, and a more relaxed attitude toward drug experimentation and abuse.

It appears that the risk of sudden death with any given episode of inhalant use exceeds that presented with any other

drug of abuse. Death has been noted to occur by a variety of cardiovascular, pulmonary, accidental, and violence-related problems. Of particular importance is death occurring when sniffing inhalants causes heart rhythm disturbances, referred to as the "sudden sniffing death" syndrome. A sniffer's risk of sudden death is significant, even with initial experimentation. In British studies of sudden death related to inhalant use, for every ten people who died from inhalants, up to three of the victims died during their first experience of using inhalants.[17]

Today more than fourteen hundred products, ranging from simple household items to industrial products, are potentially abusable as inhalants.[18] Each year manufacturers continue to create new products that have a high abuse potential.

"Inhaling volatile solvents and gases starves the body of oxygen, resulting in potential damage to the brain and nervous system," explained Alan I. Leshner, director of the National Institute on Drug Abuse. "Even first-time inhalant users run the risk of instantaneous death," Leshner added.[19]

In Great Britain, where national statistics have been recorded, one in five people who died from inhalant abuse was a first-time user.[20] In spite of the fact that inhalants result in an untold number of deaths every year, many people remain ignorant of the size and scope of this problem.

Inhalants fall into three main groups: solvents, aerosols, and nitrites and nitrous oxide. Solvents are chemicals that can dissolve or break down another substance. Aerosols are chemicals that can be sprayed. Nitrites are salts or fragrant compounds of nitrous acid.

Questions for Discussion

1. What do you think accounts for the rise in inhalant abuse?

2. What do you think is the biggest risk associated with inhalant abuse?

3. There is no central system in the United States for reporting deaths resulting from inhalant abuse. Suggest some possible reasons for this lack of tracking.

2
Poisonous Effects of Solvents

All of a sudden, a fifteen-year-old boy turns violent. He grabs a gun and begins shooting. Moments later, a thirteen-year-old girl from Oak Cliff, Texas, lies dead on the floor. In another part of the country, a fourteen-year-old boy stands on a rooftop, thinking he can fly. He starts flapping his arms and falls several stories to his death.[1]

Were these boys LSD or PCP addicts? No. They were high from inhaling paint thinner. Paint thinner is one of many solvents with high abuse potential.

What Are Solvents?

Solvents are chemicals that can dissolve or break down another substance. Volatile refers to a substance's tendency to vaporize—leave the

Poisonous Effects of Solvents

liquid state and enter the gaseous state. The amount of liquid that is vaporized is related to the solvent's particular chemical properties.[2] When volatile solvents are inhaled, the lungs quickly absorb the vapors. From the thin, moist lining of the lungs, the chemicals pass into the bloodstream and are carried to the brain, as well as other parts of the body. Exposure to solvents may cause intoxication or other physical and behavioral effects.

Why Do Sniffers Sniff?

Most people abusing an inhalant believe nothing bad is going to happen to them. For some inhalant abusers, it is the "in" thing to do. They may try inhaling out of curiosity or because of peer pressure. Often young children unintentionally misuse products that are found in the home. Many sniffers do it to make them feel high or stoned or give them a buzz. They may think it will change the way they feel about themselves.

Some people who experiment with inhalants often describe a feeling of euphoria—without a care in the world. Others abuse inhalants to escape boredom, depression, difficulties in school, and a troubled home life. Many people intentionally become caught up in the inhalant abuse scene.[3]

Patterns of Use

The pattern of inhalant abuse in the United States is shown in a national study, the annual Monitoring the Future Study conducted by the University of Michigan's Institute for Social Research for the National Institute of Drug Abuse. The 1994 report of the Monitoring the Future Study found that 35 percent of eighth-graders, almost 43 percent of tenth-graders, and almost

Inhalants

half of twelfth-graders have used illegal drugs in their lifetime, including inhalants.[4]

Breathing in the vapors from volatile solvents usually results in a rapid, yet extremely dangerous high. This is obtained in a number of ways.

Methods Used

Sniffing, or breathing fumes directly from an inhalant substance, can be done in many ways. The vapors of liquid solvents are often "sniffed" (inhaled by nose) directly from an open container. Sniffers (people who abuse inhalants in this way) may also put liquid solvents into plastic bottles or soft-drink cans from which they inhale the fumes.

To increase the concentration of the vapors and get a greater effect, liquid solvents may also be "huffed" (inhaled by mouth). The solvent is poured onto a rag or piece of clothing and held over the mouth and nose for inhalation. Emptying the product into a bag and holding the bag opening firmly over the nose and mouth is another popular method for using solvents. Huffing is also the street term used for inhalant abuse by any method.

Hazards

Other methods of increasing the effects of solvents include putting the whole head in a large plastic bag. Unfortunately this method, which increases the danger of suffocation, is often too effective and the user loses consciousness and dies. Heating a flammable solvent to concentrate the vapors is another hazardous practice. Many inhalant abusers have suffered burns from the explosion of solvents.

Unfortunately, a young person does not have to find a drug dealer, or even leave home to find inhalants. The easy availability of household products with abuse potential is a contributing factor to the widespread and dangerous use of inhalants.

Inhalants

Mike started sniffing glue in sixth-grade art class. Later, he found new ways to get high using bathroom and kitchen products. According to Mike, if the labels read "fatal if swallowed," he would try it. At the filling station where he worked, he would get high on exhaust fumes by closing the garage doors and letting an engine run for half an hour. After landing in a drug treatment program, Mike said, "I'm lucky to be alive."[5]

Why Are Certain Specific Substances Inhaled?

Some consider the odor to be important; other users believe that the feeling one gets is most important. Many inhalant abusers use one or two favorite brands, but this changes according to availability.[6] Yet sniffers do seem to go out of their way to get their preferences.

Solvents in the Body

Absorption of the solvent from the air into the body occurs first in the lungs. In seconds, the vapors enter into the bloodstream. Once in the body volatile solvents seek out fatty tissue, such as that of the brain, heart, liver, kidneys, and muscles. The solvents produce effects similar to anesthetics, acting to slow down the body's functions.

Their Effect

Since an inhaled drug moves directly to the brain, its effects are stronger than those produced by injected or swallowed substances. How strong these effects are depends on how much is inhaled and what substance is used. A single incident of solvent

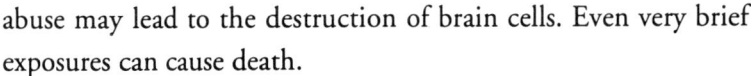

abuse may lead to the destruction of brain cells. Even very brief exposures can cause death.

A Cheap and Easy High

The inhalant-induced high is immediate and short, lasting anywhere from a few minutes to about an hour. At low doses, users may feel slightly stimulated. At moderate amounts, the user feels less inhibited, less in control, light-headed and giddy, often appearing to be drunk. Loss of consciousness and death can occur at high doses.[7]

Solvents leave the body in different ways. Many solvents are eliminated by exhaling them. Other solvents are changed into a more water-soluble form and eliminated in the urine or passed out of the body through the skin.

Adverse Effects of Use

Inhaling solvents can cause damaging poisonous or toxic effects. Many of the symptoms of the solvent abuser "resemble alcohol intoxication."[8] These substances can be lethal to people who are exposed to them in heavy concentrations or over long periods of time. Death can occur at any time—even one-time use can result in death.

"If inhalants don't kill you fast, they will kill you slowly," said Dr. Neil Rosenberg, a neurologist and medical director of the Denver-based International Institute for Inhalant Abuse. "Inhalants are some of the worst substances to abuse because they can kill you with the very first use."[9] Death can result from heart failure. The rhythmic beat of the heart is disrupted, making the muscle quiver, then stop altogether. Suffocation due to lack of oxygen in the lungs can also cause death.

Sniffing glue and other substances can cause irreversible damage to lungs, brain cells, liver, and bone marrow.

Effects on the Body

Initial effects of solvent abuse include nausea, sneezing, coughing, nosebleeds, bad breath, imbalance, dizziness, loss of appetite, the appearance and feeling of tiredness, and heart rhythm changes. Solvent abuse brings on confusion, slurred speech, a feeling of numbness, a runny nose, drunkenness, tears, headache, lack of muscular coordination, and blurred vision. Some solvents cause the user to experience hallucinations.

Abusers of glue risk having the "sniffer's rash"—an ugly reddening of the skin around the mouth. This is usually caused by the person repeatedly putting a plastic bag to the nose and mouth. In addition to red skin, the rash may consist of spots and sores, like acne. When the sniffing stops, the skin usually clears up.

Studies in England showed that long-term abuse of toluene, the chemical found in glue, caused the user to forget things, speak slowly, and not think clearly. Brain scans of glue sniffers revealed that the cortex—the part of the brain that helps people think things through and understand—had actually decreased in size.[10]

Behavioral Effects

Deep breathing of solvent vapors, or abuse of a large quantity over a short period of time, may result in losing touch with surroundings, losing self-control, behaving violently, or even becoming unconscious.

Inhalation may result in temporary numbness, distortion of space and time, and feelings of great strength, often leading to bizarre and reckless behavior.

Brian, who began huffing at age sixteen, admits that he

Inhalants

passed out a couple of times, but that was what he was aiming for—this just meant the inhalant he huffed was working. He preferred marijuana, cocaine, or LSD, but those drugs were too expensive for him. "Huffing was a good, cheap substitute. There was Wite-Out™ at school, gas or paint in the garage—it was everywhere I looked. And the high only lasted about fifteen minutes with no hangover or needle marks."[11]

Toxic Effects

Most people who abuse solvents can never be sure of what risks they are taking. Commercial products that are inhaled may contain several different solvents, each with its own toxicity.[12] For example, toluene is toxic to the nervous system only at very high levels, yet the benzene that is usually found with toluene can cause cancer at lower levels. Other solvents are also suspected of being carcinogens—substances that produce or contribute to the growth of cancer. However, benzene is the only solvent that has been thoroughly studied and linked to leukemia, a form of cancer.[13]

Fetal Solvent Syndrome

Inhaling solvents during pregnancy is a very dangerous practice because the developing fetus is especially susceptible to the effects of solvents. Some solvents have the ability to end a pregnancy. Other solvents can damage reproductive cells. Although the extent of these effects is not yet clear, preliminary studies link prenatal exposure to the solvent toulene to the following abnormalities: small head, deep-set eyes, disfigured nose and ears, stubby fingers, slow growth, shortened attention span, and damage to the nerves and kidneys.[14] These physical malformations or functional impairments have come to be known as Fetal

Solvent Syndrome. It is very similar to Fetal Alcohol Syndrome. The National Institute on Drug Abuse's 1994 National Pregnancy and Health Survey reported that approximately twelve thousand fetuses were exposed to inhalants while in the uterus.[15]

Tolerance

Repeated sniffing of solvent vapors over a period of time will likely develop a tolerance in the user. Tolerance refers to the way a person's body gradually becomes accustomed to the drug, so that its effects become less and less after repeated use. As a result, higher and higher doses are needed to achieve the same effect as the first experience. Larger doses multiply all the risks connected with inhalant abuse.

Psychological Dependence

Solvent abusers become preoccupied with the feelings they get from inhalants. Because it can interfere with physical, mental, and emotional development, psychological dependence is especially a problem for young people.

Some people will do just about anything to keep a steady supply for their habit. One user ran to a friend's house—with no clothes on—looking for glue. To try to stop him from leaving the house to look for glue, his parents had taken away his clothes.[16]

Withdrawal

When people who are physically dependent on solvents stop using, they have a withdrawal reaction. Withdrawal may result in yearning for the drug, shaking, trembling, and sweating. Withdrawal can produce many symptoms, including anxiety and depression, headaches, abdominal pains and nausea, muscle cramps,

 Inhalants

hostile outbursts, and hallucinations. These symptoms occur within hours or a few days after use stops.[17]

Effects on the Brain

Repeated sniffing of concentrated vapors of solvents over a number of years can cause brain damage. Inhalants cause users to feel high by reducing the supply of oxygen to the brain. Brain cells die if too much oxygen is cut off. Brain cells are not replaceable, so the damage is permanent. This condition creates shakes, poor coordination, and difficulty in walking. Repeat users show greatly reduced mental capabilities: poorer memory, slower responses, and a reduced ability to perform simple calculations.

Dr. Neil Rosenberg described an MRI (magnetic resonance imaging, or a kind of x ray of the brain) of a twenty-two-year-old chronic inhalant abuser as being like the brain of an eighty-year-old with Parkinson's disease. He said, "I know of no other substance that has this effect in such a short amount of time."[18]

Cardiovascular Effects

From cases of abusers dying before reaching the emergency room, researchers found that solvents can affect the normal functioning of the heart. A number of solvents are known to cause the heart to beat wildly, with no regular rhythm or pumping effect, a condition known as arrhythmia. The combination of solvent abuse and stress can overstimulate the heart, leading to elevated heart rate and blood pressure.

Other Dangers

Long-term sniffing can cause liver and kidney damage, respiratory problems, and the permanent loss of taste, feeling, hearing,

Inhalation of gasoline fumes causes dizziness and serious damage to the blood vessels of the brain and respiratory system.

 Inhalants

and smell. Over time, the abuse of solvents can lead to a reduction in the formation of blood cells in the bone marrow and long-lasting brain damage. Benzene can cause cancer. Chronic use of substances such as n-hexane—which is commonly found in gasoline, various adhesives, rubber cement, and some plastic cement—can cause permanent damage to muscles.

Other physical effects caused by chronic use of solvents are fatigue, a pale appearance, weight loss, and excessive thirst. Some of these long-term effects are reversible, but only after the user stops abusing solvents.

Questions for Discussion

1. In your opinion, why do people abuse solvents?

2. What are some of the problems with abusing solvents?

3. Suggest some strategies that can be used in the home to prevent solvent abuse.

3

The Dangers of Aerosols

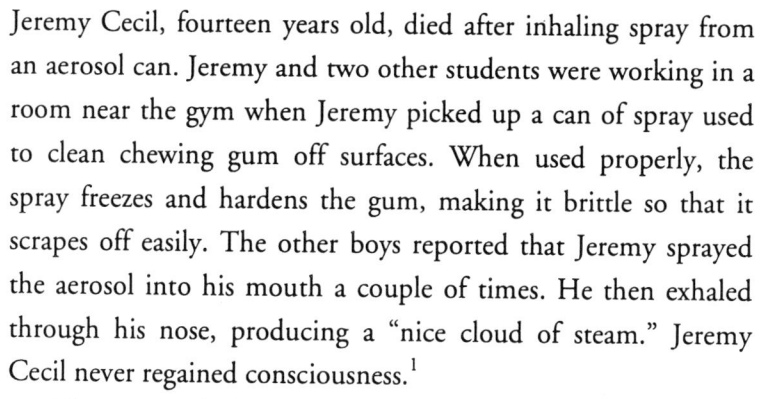

Jeremy Cecil, fourteen years old, died after inhaling spray from an aerosol can. Jeremy and two other students were working in a room near the gym when Jeremy picked up a can of spray used to clean chewing gum off surfaces. When used properly, the spray freezes and hardens the gum, making it brittle so that it scrapes off easily. The other boys reported that Jeremy sprayed the aerosol into his mouth a couple of times. He then exhaled through his nose, producing a "nice cloud of steam." Jeremy Cecil never regained consciousness.[1]

The term "inhalants" describes groups of psychoactive chemicals that are defined by how they are taken rather than by their effects on the central nervous system.[2] Anything and everything that can be sprayed is considered to be an aerosol—and they all have an exceptionally high abuse potential. Like solvents, aerosols can be found in many common household items.

Chemicals in aerosols include butane, propane, toluene, nitrous oxide, fluorocarbons, and chlorofluorocarbons. The United States banned the use of fluorocarbons for most commercial applications at the beginning of the 1980s because they contribute to pollution of the atmosphere and depletion of the ozone layer.

Abused Products

Cooking sprays, furniture polishes, fabric protector sprays, insecticides, insect repellants, air fresheners, hair sprays, deodorants, and spray medications are some of the products that have been abused. Marketable forms of fluorocarbons that are still available include pressurized refrigerant refills and asthma inhalers. Pure gas is available in pressurized containers such as butane lighters.

These products contain many different chemicals, all of which have different chemical properties. The additives in most of these aerosols are at least as poisonous as the gases themselves. These chemicals are sometimes listed on the product container. Because many products do not identify all the substances and may often refer to ingredients as "nontoxic hydrocarbons," the information on the container may be misleading. Most of these products carry warnings such as: "Intentional use by deliberately concentrating and inhaling the contents can be harmful or fatal." For the most part, these warnings are ignored by huffers.

One study of 110 inhalant-related deaths in the United States concluded that the most common substances involved were propellants from aerosols. Many of the deaths were

 Inhalants

probably caused by cardiac arrhythmia, a condition that causes the heart to beat irregularly.[3]

Patterns of Use

Breathing in the vapors from aerosol products usually provides a rapid, yet extremely dangerous high. Some abusers of aerosols spray the substance directly into their mouths for inhalation. Sometimes the spray is aimed up the nose. Many abusers prefer to separate the propellant gas from other ingredients.

One fifteen-year-old girl died after inhaling an aerosol product at an Alabama skating rink. A thirteen-year-old friend who was with her at the time described the incident: "We were just out there and a guy gave [the victim] some of the [spray] on her shirt and she smelled it and she passed out and hit her head." Her friend said, "I don't think she had ever used it before."[4]

Neurologist Dr. Neil Rosenberg said that inhalant use is like playing Russian roulette. "You might huff a certain amount one time and be fine. The next time out, that same amount will kill."[5]

Toluene

Toluene is a flammable colorless liquid. It is the intoxicant in many aerosols, including spray paint. It is also used to make other paints, perfumes, medicines, dyes, explosives, and detergents. The chemical can damage the liver, kidneys, brain, and bone marrow. Toluene saturates fatty tissues which include the brain, the fattiest organ. The myelin sheath, a covering of nerve endings, is another high-fat part. Both are subject to abuse. Because of its ability to permeate, toluene gets into the nervous system within "a matter of a few moments," said Rosenberg.[6] In addition to permanent brain damage, toluene may cause blindness, deafness, coma—and death.

Evidence suggests that toluene can cause permanent damage to developing fetuses. Dr. Pat O'Meara, director of newborn services at Denver General Hospital, has been present at births where the amniotic fluid, which surrounds the fetus in the uterus, smells of toluene. "The baby just bathed in it inside."[7]

Spray paint, especially gold or silver paint, is a popular inhalant. "If you're a true connoisseur of paint, you go for the gold," said one police officer.[8] Sniffers prefer gold spray paint because of the sweet taste it leaves, rather than the bitter taste produced by clear paint.

One young man was addicted to the toxic vapors given off by copper and gold paint. He inhaled the fumes from a bread bag held around his face. The inhalation left its mark, staining his face to match the colors of the substances he breathed. On the street, police knew him by his nickname—David Copperfield.[9]

One nineteen-year-old huffed spray paint, hoping to get high. While experiencing the expected high, he failed to see an approaching train as he crossed the railroad tracks. He died instantly.[10]

Butane

Donovan C. Baker, eighteen years old, died of cardiac arrest at his home. He and several other teens had been inhaling butane lighter refills. His mother, Jackie Baker, said that he and his friends were not aware that butane can be lethal. He had told his younger brother that it was not illegal and it could not hurt you. Prior to his death, his mother had noticed that her son's eyes were glassy and his pupils dilated. When questioned, he explained it away.[11]

Huffing: The breath of death

Butane, a compressed, odorless gas, is sold in canisters about the size of hair spray or spray-paint cans. The chemical is used for refueling cigarette lighters. Inhaling butane often causes a brief high, followed by blacking out.

Butane also poses a fire hazard. Kitty Lyons and three of her friends bought two canisters of butane. They huffed those, and then bought two more from a different store. They drove to a school parking lot and inhaled the other two canisters. When they finished with the cans, they tossed them out of the car.

One of the four teens then lit a cigarette. The spark from the cigarette lighter ignited the chemical still in the air, causing an explosion in their car that lasted only a fraction of a second. However, during that time, the temperature in the car rose to nearly 3000° F. Kitty and her friends ended up in the hospital with severe burns on their faces and upper bodies.[12] They were lucky to have survived.

Many parents have never heard of inhaling butane until after their child's injury or death. Janet Griffie's sixteen-year-old son Michael died after inhaling butane. Michael and a friend stopped at a convenience store and bought two cans of butane. According to police reports, Michael vomited and lost consciousness after huffing some of the butane. His friend drove him home. Michael's parents called paramedics, but it was too late.

Janet Griffie had warned her son about the dangers of hard drugs, such as marijuana and cocaine, but she had not heard of inhalants until about a year prior to her son's death. "His heart just stopped after he used that stuff," she said.[13]

A South Carolina college student had been sniffing air freshener during the hours leading up to his death. Authorities ruled that he suffered butane poisoning. Toxicology tests found butane gas, an ingredient in the air freshener, in his bloodstream.[14]

A fifteen-year-old girl, whose car ran off the road and killed two children in a hit-and-run accident, explained to the court that she was so high she never knew what she hit. Before driving a car that day in September 1992, she had inhaled butane.[15]

Freon

Freon™ is a trade name for any of a series of gases used as refrigerants and propellants in aerosol products. Freon is used in older automobile air conditioners and to recharge air conditioners. Refrigerants belong to a family of compounds known as chlorofluorocarbons (CFCs). The Clean Air Act, signed into law on November 15, 1990, is aimed at controlling substances released into the atmosphere. It is now illegal to purchase refrigerants without proof of proper training and certification.[16] Also, Freon is no longer being used in newer model cars' air conditioning units.

Joanne Begley stopped on the way home from work and picked up sandwiches for her family. When she entered the house, she called out for her nineteen-year-old son—but there was no response. Her son was lying on the floor of his room. He was not moving. The coroner's office ruled that Mark J. Begley died from inhaling Freon.

The victim's mother acknowledged there were subtle signs that her son might be troubled. At one time she had him tested for drug use. "I never dreamed it would be anything like freon. I thought maybe marijuana or alcohol. Not this."[17]

Mental health experts refer to freon abuse as hitching on to the "Death Ride." The quick-acting thirty-second high produced

Sniffing things such as markers or spray paint can kill—the first time, the second time, *any* time.

by inhaling Freon can cause unconsciousness for five to thirty minutes.[18] One sniff can cause instant death.

A sixteen-year-old Utah boy's mother found him dead in his room. A bottle of compressed refrigerant was nearby. The Freon used by the boy was a thirty-pound canister used in household refrigerators. His sister told police, "He liked to do it because it made him pass out."[19]

Propane

Propane is another pressurized gas used by inhalant abusers for a cheap, quick high. Inhaling propane often seems harmless to the user until a death occurs.

For one fifteen-year-old girl, it started out like an ordinary Saturday night—hanging out at a friend's house with several classmates. According to one friend, she popped outside twice for a "huff" and came back inside a couple of minutes later. The third time she failed to return.

Several teens rushed outside when they heard a thump. The girl was on the deck, unconscious, the hose of a propane tank by her side.

Jennifer Leigh Hoover died of cardiac arrest on November 6, 1993, after inhaling propane gas from an outdoor grill. Her parents did not see it coming. They had talked to Jennifer about illegal drugs. She always responded that she would not do anything like that. She even belonged to her high school chapter of Students Against Drugs.

The friend, who drove Jennifer to the house that ill-fated night, said Jennifer liked propane because it made her laugh. "I don't think she knew it could kill her."[20]

Decongestant Sprays

An addiction related to inhalant abuse is the dependency on nasal or asthma decongestant sprays. Asthma spray is one of the few marketable forms of fluorocarbons, other than the pressurized refrigerant refills used for air conditioning, available to the public.

With repeated and extended use, some people become physically dependent on these drugs to the point that when they stop using the decongestant sprays they have difficulty breathing, whether or not they are physically sick. To breathe normally, they need an increasing supply of the spray.

This physical dependence is known as the rebound phenomenon. Patients who abuse nasal sprays can be treated with small amounts of steroids.[21]

How Do Aerosols Work?

The inhaled vapors from aerosols pass directly from the lungs into the bloodstream and then into the brain within seconds. Intoxication is immediate. Whether the fumes come from butane, propane, or the aerosol nozzle on a spray product, they produce feelings of giddiness and euphoria, a "spacey" sensation.

The effects of aerosol abuse are often unpredictable. They depend on how the person felt beforehand, the mood of the group, and if the user has eaten a meal recently. The body's breathing and heart rate slow down. Inhalation produces sleepiness, numbness, slurred speech, a clumsy walk, and a feeling of not knowing where you are. More inhalation leads to "crashing out" or becoming unconscious. Some aerosols cause hallucinations, which can result in bizarre and reckless behavior as well as fear and anxiety.

Abandoned buildings provide unsupervised havens for sniffers.

Harmful Effects

Depending on the substance inhaled, users may experience effects ranging from memory loss to permanent brain damage. Besides brain damage from oxygen deprivation, some aerosols "coat" the lungs and can cause respiratory damage or suffocation. The chemicals in aerosol products can cause pneumonia and kidney failure. Users can appear intoxicated and lose consciousness.

Some aerosol propellants under pressure are extremely cold when released from the container. These fumes, when sprayed directly into the mouth from an aerosol, can freeze the voice box, throat, and lungs. This could be followed by swelling and suffocation.[22]

Sudden Sniffing Death

After the initial reports of propellant abuse, follow-up reports from hospitals indicated that inhalation of some substances, including propellants, can result in instant death. From cases of abusers dying even before reaching the hospital, researchers determined that inhalants affect the normal functioning of the heart.[23] This syndrome is known as Sudden Sniffing Death (SSD) because it strikes so fast. It can happen the first time a person experiments with inhalants or after years of abuse.[24] Death caused by deliberately inhaling aerosol propellants for the purpose of getting high was first reported in 1970.[25]

> **SSD is caused by several factors:**
>
> - *Inhalants act directly on the brain, decreasing the amount of oxygen supplied to the brain and the rest of the body.*

- *The oxygen supply is further decreased due to the inhalation of a chemical instead of air.*
- *Increased sensitivity of the heart muscle to the body's own adrenaline occurs, leading to an irregular heartbeat and diminished ability of the heart to pump blood and oxygen to the brain.*
- *Any excitement, such as running, sudden motion, fear, or anger, causes the body to release more adrenaline than it normally would.*[26]

In April 1990, a fifteen-year-old boy was found unconscious in a backyard in Cincinnati, Ohio. "Three companions related that the four teenagers had taken a twenty-gallon propane tank from the family gas grill, placed some of the gas in a plastic bag and were inhaling it in order to get high. They also tried 'torch breathing.' They intentionally exhaled the propane gas and ignited it." The victim collapsed soon after inhaling the gas. The fumes, ignited by a match, resulted in a flash fire; however, the victim was not burned. He could not be brought back to life though, and died before reaching the hospital.[27]

Long-term Dangers of Extensive Usage

Chronic use of aerosols leads to shrinkage of the brain and damage to the liver and kidneys.

Other physical effects of long-term use include weight loss, fatigue, and excessive thirst. People who abuse aerosols may have difficulty urinating, reduced motor coordination, or bizarre thoughts and behavior.

When people abuse inhalants more than twice a week, the substance builds up in their systems. Most of the time, it takes many weeks for some chemicals to clear out of a user's bloodstream or body organs. Experts doubt that the damage to heavy users can be repaired.

Clinical counselor Robin Beaudrot of Charleston, South Carolina, said "those who don't die from abusing inhalants may suffer long-term emotional, physical, and psychological effects."[28]

Questions for Discussion

1. Do you think makers of aerosol products should do more to prevent inhalant abuse?

2. What factors contribute to Sudden Sniffing Death (SSD)?

3. Why do you think inhalants are often referred to as the entry or "gateway" drugs to other drug use?

4
Amyl Nitrite, Butyl Nitrite, and Nitrous Oxide

For thousands of years, nitrite, present as an impurity in salt, was a key ingredient in curing meats. Many foods are naturally rich in nitrites. Combined with other chemicals called amides or amines, nitrites can form a family of compounds called nitrosamines. As a group, these substances are among the most powerful cancer-causing agents known. Nitrosamines are not permitted to be knowingly added to food at any level. In 1978, the Food and Drug Administration (FDA) set the maximum amount of nitrites that could be added to bacon.[1]

In recent years, amyl nitrite and butyl nitrite have become popular in certain circles. These are not the typical inhalants previously described. The individuals who primarily abuse nitrites are usually a different group from those who abuse other inhalants.[2] Amyl nitrite is a prescription drug used by heart patients. The effects of butyl nitrite are similar to those of amyl nitrite, but butyl nitrite is not considered to be a drug and is marketed as a "room odorizer."

Both amyl and butyl nitrite are known for the speed and intensity of their effects. The nitrite rush is almost instantaneous and lasts only a few seconds, causing users to inhale more and more of the chemicals. Nitrites have been used by people who believe that nitrites enhance sexual experience. However, researchers have not found any data to prove this.[3]

Amyl Nitrite

Amyl nitrite has been used medically since 1967 to treat heart patients. It dilates or opens the blood vessels and makes the heart beat faster. This clear, yellowish liquid is sold in mesh-covered or cloth-covered glass capsules, originally called pearls. Amyl nitrite inhalants are known on the street as "poppers"—a name derived from the sound of crushing the small vial between the fingers.[4] When snapped or broken open, a sweet, fruity vapor is released and inhaled immediately.

In spite of the drug's wide range of poison levels, the Food and Drug Administration (FDA) eliminated the prescription requirement for amyl nitrite in September 1960. Reports of recreational use of amyl nitrite were made in the early 1960s.[5] Following testimony presented by the pharmaceutical industry regarding significant abuse of amyl nitrite, the FDA put the prescription requirement back in force in 1969. The FDA's regulation did not stop the abuse of the drug, however. During

Chemicals Commonly Found in Inhalants

ADHESIVES
airplane glue	toluene, ethyl acetate
PVC cement	trichloroethylene
rubber cement	hexane, toluene, methyl chloride, acetone, methyl ethyl ketone, methyl butyl ketone

AEROSOLS
air fresheners	butane, propane (U.S.), flourocarbons
analgesic spray	flourocarbons
asthma spray	flourocarbons
deodorants	butane, propane (U.S.), flourocarbons
hair sprays	butane, propane (U.S.), flourocarbons
paint sprays	hydrocarbons, toluene

ANESTHETICS
gaseous	nitrous oxide
liquid	halothane, enflurane
local	ethyl chloride

CLEANING AGENTS
degreasers	tetrachloroethylene, trichloroethane, trichloroethylene
dry cleaning	tetrachloroethylene, trichloroethane
spot removers	tetrachloroethylene, trichloroethane, trichloroethylene

FOOD PRODUCTS
whipped cream	nitrous oxide
Whippets	nitrous oxide

SOLVENTS
correction fluid thinners	trichloroethylene, trichloroethane
fire extinguisher	bromochlorodifluoromethane
fuel gas	butane
lighter	butane, isopropane
paint remover	toluene, methylene chloride, methanol
paint thinners	toluene, methylene chloride, methanol
polish remover	acetone

the years 1974 to 1977 the popper craze really began. By 1979, studies found that more than 5 million people in the United States used the drug more than once a week.[6]

Amyl nitrite acts as a short-term heart stimulant. It also dilates the blood vessels in the body. Inhaled amyl nitrite increases the heart rate and causes a drop in blood pressure. The drug shuts off oxygen to the brain, producing a sudden intense weakness and dizzy sensation lasting thirty to sixty seconds.

As a street drug, poppers were often used on social occasions to promote a sense of freedom while dancing, to stimulate music appreciation, and to enhance meditation. On a more general basis, amyl nitrite inhalants were used to obtain an altered state of consciousness.

During the late nineteenth and early twentieth centuries, amyl nitrite was used to treat angina pectoris, a painful heart condition. It is still available today for relief of angina pectoris. It is also used for diagnostic purposes in heart examinations and in the treatment for cyanide poisoning.[7]

Butyl Nitrite

Butyl nitrite was investigated in the late 1880s. Although it contains the same properties as amyl nitrite, it was never used clinically. When amyl nitrite passed back from over-the-counter status to prescription-only status in 1969, butyl nitrite became a popular substitute. Butyl nitrite does not fit the definition of a food, drug, or cosmetic as specified by the Federal Food, Drug, and Cosmetic Act, so the FDA has no control over its use. This means that butyl nitrite is not subject to regulation by the FDA.[8] Even though it has no clinical or practical use, it is widely available in bars, in boutiques, and through mail orders.

Amyl Nitrite, Butyl Nitrite, and Nitrous Oxide

Butyl nitrite was not covered by the Food and Drug Act in Canada until 1985. Since the sale of butyl nitrite has been made illegal in Canada, studies indicate that Canadian use has dropped substantially. However, this does not prevent abusers from purchasing nitrites in some states adjacent to Canada.[9]

Packaged in small bottles or aerosol cans, butyl nitrite is available over the counter as a "room odorizer" or "incense." It has an unpleasant chemical odor, resembling sweaty socks or the smell of a gym locker room. It is sold under a variety of street names such as "locker room," "rush," or "medusa." It has become a popular drug of abuse among American teenagers looking for a cheap, quick thrill.

Minutes before the car crash that claimed her life, eighteen-year-old Martha Deanne Wright and two friends, both of whom survived, had taken "hits" from an aerosol can of butyl nitrite.

On that fateful night, Martha climbed into her small Toyota with a fifteen-year-old girlfriend and Kevin, twenty, another longtime friend. They drove to a store for the sole purpose of buying an aromatic spray that the three had been told would bring a safe high. They sprayed the substance, which contained butyl nitrite, on the sleeves of their clothing, wrapped their mouths around the moist fabric and inhaled. They took another hit as they traveled down a freeway.

Martha's car rammed into the back of a Cadillac and then crossed over into the lane of an oncoming pick-up truck, causing a second crash. Reports of the fatality indicated that this was the only time Martha Wright had used a drug.[10]

Short-term Problems Linked to Amyl and Butyl Nitrites

Amyl nitrite differs from butyl nitrite in legal classification, but the effects are basically the same. Inhalation of high concentrations of nitrites produces a brief surge of dizziness, a drop in blood pressure, relaxation of muscles, and a fluttering heart rate followed by sweating and flushing. These effects are accompanied by throbbing headaches and nausea. Inhaling either amyl or butyl nitrite can cause a rapid pulse and a lack of control over urination and bowel movements.[11]

Blackouts occur, particularly if the user is also drinking alcohol or using other drugs, and can cause a fall or injury. Danger also exists for anyone with defective blood vessels. If the vessels are not able to handle the sudden widening caused by inhalation of nitrites, death is the result.[12]

Risks of Long-term Use of Nitrites

Skin contact with butyl nitrite can produce a crusty sore at the site. Frequent use of the substance can lead to sores around the nose and lip.

Nitrites increase pressure in the nerves and blood vessels within the eyes. This may lead to glaucoma, an eye disorder that can cause blindness.[13]

Nitrites damage red blood cells and may cause fatal anemia when the abuser's blood can no longer transport oxygen. This happens most often to users who swallow rather than sniff.

Although awareness of negative health effects of nitrite abuse was raised in the 1970s, real concern surfaced with the Acquired Immunodeficiency Syndrome (AIDS) epidemic. Studies have

A cheap thrill can lead to deadly consequences.

linked the use of nitrite inhalants to the development of Kaposi's sarcoma, the most common cancer reported among AIDS patients. Early studies showed that many people with Kaposi's sarcoma, a cancer of the blood vessels, had used nitrites.[14] Researchers are continuing to investigate the possibility of nitrites contributing to the development of Kaposi's sarcoma in HIV-infected people.

Nitrous Oxide

This substance has a long medical history as a mild anesthetic. "Laughing gas," as it is popularly called, was abused soon after it was discovered in the late eighteenth century.[15] Inhaling nitrous oxide for pleasure is still practiced today. It is abused by young people, as well as by people in the medical profession.

Nitrous oxide is a colorless, sweet-smelling gas that produces giddiness, a dreamy or floating sensation, and a mild, pain-free state. Because it relieves anxiety and indirectly blocks pain, it is used for minor oral surgery and dental work.

Sources of Nitrous Oxide

Nitrous oxide is sold in large tanks that can be bought only with a license. The large tanks can be purchased from industrial distributors for use as propellants or from auto-racing shops as a pre-ignition booster. Many abusers steal the tanks or buy them illegally. The gas is also sold in large tanks for use in medicine and dentistry.

Many believe that the recreational use of nitrous oxide is increasing partly because the gas is sold in the carnival-like marketplace of rock concerts. Dealers set up nitrous oxide tanks at

Amyl Nitrite, Butyl Nitrite, and Nitrous Oxide

rock concerts and sell balloons filled with the gas. Maryland State Police Trooper William Bonnell said, "I went undercover at a concert, and I couldn't believe nitrous oxide was so open and blatant."[16]

The best known source of nitrous oxide is whipped cream canisters. The gas is used as a propellant in whipped cream dispensers to delay spoilage. Cartridges of nitrous oxide, the size of throwaway cigarette lighters, are manufactured and sold without restriction. They are used as a part of small machines to make whipped cream, primarily in restaurants. The small cartridges, called Whippet™ Chargers, are readily available at gourmet food stores, boutiques, novelty stores, and from mail-order companies.

William Caumer, an executive at a chemical products manufacturer and chairman of an industry task force on nitrous oxide said, "It's one of the toughest products to control. By and large, there isn't much police can do." The task force is trying to draft a law that states can use to restrict distribution and use of the gas.[17]

What Whippets do:

- *Impair motor functions*

- *Kill brain cells*

- *Cause short blackouts*

- *Produce giggles*

- *Can cause suffocation*

In Cleveland, Ohio, a man under the influence of nitrous oxide ran over and killed a sixteen-month-old child in a stroller.[18] In Alexandria, Virginia, a man high on nitrous oxide blacked out after inhaling the gas and ran a red light, killing two women. He was sentenced to twenty years in prison for manslaughter.[19]

Risks Associated With Nitrous Oxide Use

Symptoms of exposure to high levels of nitrous oxide include numbness and weakness in the limbs, loss of strength, deadening of the senses, and imbalance. Animal studies for alcohol dependence on selectively bred mice showed a cross-dependency on nitrous oxide.

Probably the biggest risk involves inhaling the gas straight from pressurized tanks or masks. Researchers at the Medical College of Virginia found that nitrous-filled tanks pose the following potential serious risks to users:

- *Very cold temperatures of nitrous oxide can freeze the lips and throat.*
- *High levels of pressure may cause the lungs to collapse.*
- *Nausea, vomiting, and disorientation can occur, particularly when inhaling large amounts quickly.*
- *A temporary loss of coordination can occur.*
- *Lack of oxygen can cause brain damage and death from suffocation.*[20]

Questions For Discussion

1. Do you think the sale of butyl nitrite should be regulated by the FDA? Why or why not?

2. What are the risks of long-term use of nitrites?

3. What makes nitrous oxide one of the toughest products to control?

5
Social Aspects of Inhalant Abuse

According to Dr. Milton Tenenbein, who is a pediatrician and a toxicologist (a doctor who studies the effects of poisons on the body) in Winnipeg, Manitoba, Canada, "a lack of awareness of the significance of inhalant abuse permeates all levels of society, including government."[1] Charles Sharp, chief of the biomedical branch of the National Institute on Drug Abuse, acknowledged that inhalants have not been recognized as having a wide effect on crime or public health. As a result, only limited federal funds are used to study the problem.[2]

Role Society Plays in Inhalant Abuse

Inhalant abuse impacts families and communities. There is little awareness in society about the dangers and seriousness of the problem, according to Hugh Young, director of the Solvent Abuse Foundation for Education. Young believes inhalant abuse has received little attention because it has been stereotyped as a problem restricted to Hispanics in isolated neighborhoods or Native American populations on reservations. According to him, the inhalant problem has never been limited to any one class of society. "There are upper-class white kids who sniff and die all over this country."[3]

Harvey Weiss, chairman of the National Inhalant Prevention Coalition, agreed that in the past, inhalant abuse was perceived to be a problem of Native Americans or Mexicans. "But more and more we're finding that the fastest-growing inhalant abusers are your Anglo middle-class and upper-class kids, with females using at about the same rate as males."[4] There is mounting evidence that sniffing is cutting across racial, economic, and regional lines.

Settings and opportunities for inhalant abuse include:

- *Easy access to substances*
- *Unsupervised parties and other social events*
- *Lack of family communication*
- *Lack of family supervision*
- *Lack of curfews*
- *Lack of control by the community or by law enforcement officials of vacant lots or other places where loitering or drug abuse is known to take place*[5]

Inhalants

Matt Breen experienced his first high when he was twelve. He inhaled Liquid Paper™ fumes. "I would do Liquid Paper™ in class," Matt said. "I would put a little on notebook paper and would sniff it. I liked the attention from kids who asked me what I was doing. I knew it killed brain cells big time, but my attitude was I really didn't care. I just liked the feeling."

Typical of white middle-class users, Matt began using other drugs. In the three and a half years between his first drug use and ending up in a long-term treatment program, he went from sniffing gasoline, paint thinner, lacquer, and other inhalants to abusing marijuana and alcohol.

The first time he inhaled gasoline, Matt remembered feeling that he could not breathe, as if his chest and throat were closing in. It scared him, but he kept on sniffing in spite of the loss of balance and severe headaches. "I kept doing more and more," Matt said, "I don't know why."[6]

Why should society be concerned about inhalant use?

- *Inhalants can kill.*
- *They are a "gateway" to other drug use.*
- *They have serious consequences for youth, whose bodies and minds are in a critical maturation period.*
- *Available products surround young people.*[7]

Social Factors Underlining Inhalant Abuse

One twelve-year-old boy was found sniffing dry-cleaning fluid alone in his room. He explained that he was doing it because he had been told that people saw things when they sniffed dry-cleaning fluid. He longed to see his mother again. She had died two years before.[8]

Weakened Parental Influence

One research finding points to the idea that inhalant abusers' families may be dysfunctional. Abusers can come from broken homes, from families with conflict and discord, and from families marked by a history of alcohol or drug problems or both.

Studies looking at family drug or alcohol use indicated that the families of inhalant abusers tended to include substance abusers. Inhalant users coming from drug-abusing families had used more types of drugs, saw their friends accepting drug use, were extremely poor, and were likely to have parents who had been arrested.[9]

"For some it's part of a lifelong pattern. Parents do it. Kids do it. It's a family thing," said Jim Hall, the executive director of a drug information center in Miami that researches drug-abuse patterns and trends.[10] As family communication and closeness deteriorate, research shows, the tendency for young people to abuse inhalants increases. A large number of inhalant users report having siblings or friends who also abuse inhalants. Abuse can also be generational, with everyone in the same household, from grandparents down to grandchildren, abusing drugs.

Peer Pressure

Strong peer pressure influences inhalant abuse.[11] One stereotype of the inhalant abuser is that of the social "loner." Research reports describe most inhalant use as a group activity. Although many factors can affect inhalant abuse, researchers emphasize that the peer group is almost always one of them. The kinds of friends that inhalant abusers have may be an important factor in inhalant abuse.

Lack of Information of the Dangers of Inhalant Abuse

Lack of accurate and consistent information of the dangers of inhalant abuse contributes to the growing problem of huffing and sniffing. "Youngsters don't fully understand the lethal potential of using such substances as butane, solvents, glues, and nitrous oxide," said social psychologist Lloyd D. Johnston, Ph.D., of the University of Michigan, which conducts an annual survey of almost fifty thousand eighth-grade through twelfth-grade students.[12]

Experts say that because the substances are not illegal, many young people believe they are not harmful. "I think the main problem is authorities are very preoccupied with alcohol, marijuana, and crack cocaine, and inhalants have not been taken seriously enough," noted Evelyn McFeaters, associate director of communications with the Chemical Specialities Manufacturing Association.[13] Yet, according to the 1994 Monitoring the Future Study, inhalants are the *third* most abused substance after alcohol and tobacco among elementary and middle school students. Inhalants are the *fourth* most abused substance, after alcohol, tobacco, and marijuana, among high school students.

Parents can be unknowing suppliers for inhalant abuse because of the legal products with the potential for abuse found throughout the house, the garage, or the workshop. Before speaking to a parent group in Memphis, Tennessee, Jane Chittick, a member of the National Inhalant Prevention Coalition, decided to go through her house—looking in kitchen cabinets, under the kitchen sink, in the bathrooms, and in the garage—in search of items with abuse potential. In less than ten minutes she had filled a large plastic bag.[14]

Linda Warren came home from work and found the screen door latched. She broke in and found her twelve-year-old daughter Eve lying face down on her bed, dead. The seventh grader had overdosed by inhaling concentrated fumes from an aerosol can.

Mother and daughter were both musicians and performed at local events. Eve played saxophone and clarinet, sang in the church choir, and loved roses and her pet bird. She was a quiet, introspective child. According to her mother, she had been coming home saying, "Mama, nobody likes me."

Warren said that she had been very hard on Eve the month before she died because she was going to get a scholarship in band. "For Christmas, I got her a very expensive saxophone, but I gave it to her in October." She tried to get Eve to practice an hour a day at her grandmother's house.

Linda Warren admitted that she was at a breaking point, paying so much money on Eve's music lessons. And Eve would not practice. "But I didn't realize she couldn't practice because she didn't have any breath left."

A few weeks prior to Eve's death, her grandmother had noticed she was spending a lot of time in the bathroom and using an unusual amount of hair spray. Warren recalled that her own large supply of hair spray had been disappearing.

Warren revealed that she was ignorant of the signs and symptoms of inhalant abuse, and her daughter was not a child one would suspect of using drugs. "Eve wouldn't have thought

SNIFFING SPRAY PAINT DESTROYS YOUR LUNGS.

Studies show that one in every five or six students in grades eight through twelve have tried inhalants.

hair spray was a drug or that it was very harmful or fatal if inhaled," said her mother.[15]

Bob Kustra, lieutenant governor of Illinois, wrote to newspaper columnist Ann Landers alerting readers "to a relatively unknown but deadly problem in drug abuse among young teens—inhalants." He referred to the 1994 University of Michigan study that showed one in every five or six students in grades eight through twelve has tried inhalants. He concluded the letter, which ran in hundreds of newspapers across the country, with: "Parents should talk to their children BEFORE it becomes a problem. In spite of all we hear about outside influences, parents are still the biggest influence in the lives of young teens."[16] This means parents need to become educated.

Inhalants are often downplayed in drug education. Drug Abuse Resistance Education (DARE) is a police-run program, starting in fifth and sixth grades. The DARE program began in 1983 in Los Angeles and has spread all over the country. However, the curriculum does not always address inhalant abuse.[17]

Teachers need to be made aware of the growing problems in inhalant abuse that occur in schools. After a presentation at a junior high school by Richard Farias, director of the Association for the Advancement of Mexican Americans, one teacher was honest enough to tell him she had no idea that students were abusing correction fluid. She admitted that she had lost or given away nine bottles of Liquid Paper™ in the preceding month. "That type of unawareness permeates the schools," Farias said.[18]

Societal Trends

The 1994 University of Michigan study conducted for the National Institute on Drug Abuse noted that the recent increases in the use of inhalants, marijuana, LSD, and stimulants are not just concentrated in large cities or particular regions of the country. They are occurring across most sectors of society.

Disturbing trends include:

- *A spirit of rebellion against parents and authority*
- *Increased abuse as young people perceive substances to be less dangerous*
- *Relative increases in the use of substances with greater sudden death potential*
- *Increased inhalant use among females*
- *Increased use in settings associated with youth violence*[19]

Inhaling is becoming socially acceptable. According to studies, one of the most important factors is peer pressure. Inhalant abuse often starts with one individual and quickly spreads to others through peer-group influence.

Inhalants are considered by many authorities to be "gateway" drugs, leading to other forms of illicit drug abuse. Because they are made and used for legal purposes, easy to get, inexpensive, and difficult to detect, inhalants are often the first substance young people try. Studies show that most inhalant abusers are now between eight and eighteen years of age.[20]

A Ball State University study shows that, at all grade levels, parents have little or no perception that their children have abused inhalants.

Nationally acclaimed authority in the field of substance abuse, David J. Wilmes, of the Johnston Institute, stated that "we have raised a generation of kids whose parents don't say no to them." Parental permissiveness allows and encourages children to develop patterns of irresponsible behavior. According to Wilmes, parents do their children a disservice by protecting them from consequences, taking on their responsibilities, and lowering standards of conduct to levels that are inconsistent with their own values and beliefs.[21]

Messages Sent by Society

The values and beliefs of a nation play a significant role in substance abuse. "Taking something" to make you feel better is an accepted form of behavior in modern society. Inhalants provide a chemical shortcut to achieving satisfaction quickly and easily. There is widespread acceptance of taking substances to experience pleasure and relieve pain.[22]

Inhalants may have replaced crack cocaine as the preferred drug of the 1990s. "What we're seeing is that teens might be getting the message that crack can be incredibly, physically addictive," said Dr. Marylyn Broman, the director of adolescent medicine at the University of Miami School of Medicine. "They're thinking this stuff isn't as dangerous. It's ignorance on their part."[23]

The lack of clear punishments for inhalant abuse is also an important factor in its abuse. Researchers find the change in attitude toward substance abuse as disturbing as the increasing numbers of drug users. Fewer students disapprove of substance abuse and fewer see it as hazardous. Experts agree that the erosion in antidrug attitudes among teens is disturbing. "If kids continue to see drugs as less dangerous and more socially acceptable, use may continue to rise," explained Steve Dnistrian,

No school today? A significant amount of inhalant use occurs when the user is alone.

vice president of the Partnership for a Drug-Free America (PDFA).[24]

"These changes would worry me less if the underlying attitudes and beliefs were not also continuing to shift in the direction" of being favorable to drug use, Lloyd D. Johnston said.[25] Johnston believes the continuing rise in drug use is linked to the message that young people are getting today. "They are hearing much less about the dangers of drugs and seeing more glamorization of drugs."[26]

Questions for Discussion

1. Why does society need to be concerned about the dangers of inhalant abuse?

2. What factors contribute to the erosion of antidrug attitudes among young people?

3. What do you think the role of parents should be in combating substance abuse?

6
Personal Aspects of Inhalant Abuse

People from all walks of life abuse inhalants. Surveys and medical examiners' reports strongly indicate that inhalant abuse is not limited to any one type of person. However, in some communities, there are ethnically centered concentrations of abuse among Hispanics and Native Americans. African Americans are least likely to use inhalants, although there are those who do.[1] Whether your skin is black, red, white, or brown, inhalant abuse can affect you. Inhalant abuse cuts across racial, ethnic, economic, and geographic boundaries.

Who Uses Inhalants?

In the cities of poor countries around the world, gangs of homeless children roam the streets. Thousands are strung out on glue and other inhalants.[2] Reports of inhalant abuse come from Mexico, many European and African countries, and a number of Central and South American nations. Even the Australian aborigines and the Native Americans of arctic Manitoba are not exempt from the problem.[3] Japan and Sweden have described problems with paint thinners among juveniles. In Mexico and Australia, the number-one inhalant abused by adolescents is gasoline. In England, solvent-based glues and refills for butane lighters are usually the drugs of choice. In Canada, spray paint and typewriter correction fluid are often abused.[4] In Latin-American cities, hundreds of thousands of street children are known to use inhalants to get high. Inhalant abuse is a serious problem throughout the world.

Children

One fifteen-year-old Kansas City boy in drug treatment said that he began sniffing gasoline when he was eight years old. "The first time I did it, I was smelling gas from the lawn mower, and I fell asleep with my nose on the gas tank," he said. Soon after, he began sniffing lighter fluid, spray paint, and cement remover to achieve the same high.

"When the gas wasn't around, I would sit and think about what was in the house that I could use," he recalled. "I'd think there was nothing around, but then I'd remember, 'Oh, yeah, we have that.'"

The boy's habit expanded to include marijuana by the time he was twelve years old. In his opinion, inhalant use is more harmful than other drugs. "I thought what I was doing was fun and cool, but I can't remember things as well anymore."[5]

A curious first-time sniffer may not get a second chance.

Inhalants may be the least expensive, least known, and least talked-about class of chemical substances, but they are the class of drugs most commonly abused by very young children—those age eleven and under.[6] The National Institute on Drug Abuse reported that children as young as seven years of age are likely to abuse inhalants because they are cheap, available legally, and very convenient.

Younger siblings are influenced by their older brothers and sisters and by what they see going on around them. Seeing others use drugs heightens their curiosity and their willingness to try something new.[7]

A counselor at a Minneapolis adolescent detox center thought he had seen a lot as a counselor, but nothing prepared him for one of his patients. The boy was no older than nine. "When he walked out into the hallway, there was nothing there but pajamas with a little head on top," said the counselor. "Here was a kid who should have been riding his bike or playing in the park. Instead he was there."[8]

A nationwide survey by PRIDE, an Atlanta-based national drug education group, found that 29 percent of students reported that they had started using inhalants before their tenth birthday.[9]

There is growing concern about secondhand inhalant abuse. Adults who abuse inhalants run the risk of forcing their children to inhale the fumes—either in the womb when pregnant women huff or in the air of their homes.

Teens

The abuse of inhalants—which has been rising since the early 1980s—is highest during early adolescence. Generally, inhalant abuse peaks around eighth grade or age thirteen. "It is a problem

Lifetime Drug Use of Young Adults

Percentage of eighth graders, tenth graders, and twelfth graders using inhalants, marijuana, and illicit drugs in their lifetimes:

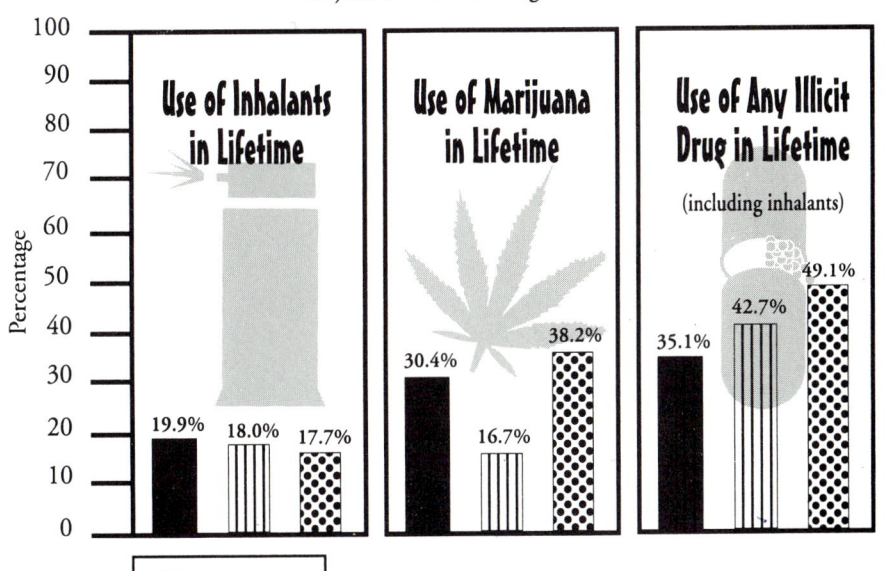

Use of Inhalants in Lifetime
- eighth graders: 19.9%
- tenth graders: 18.0%
- twelfth graders: 17.7%

Use of Marijuana in Lifetime
- eighth graders: 16.7%
- tenth graders: 30.4%
- twelfth graders: 38.2%

Use of Any Illicit Drug in Lifetime
(including inhalants)
- eighth graders: 35.1%
- tenth graders: 42.7%
- twelfth graders: 49.1%

Legend:
- twelfth graders
- tenth graders
- eighth graders

Source: The Monitoring the Future Study, University of Michigan, 1994.

which is getting worse at a fairly rapid pace," said Lloyd D. Johnston, Ph.D.[10] Also troubling is the rapid increase of inhalant use by young girls. The rates of inhalant abuse for males and females have been getting closer together over the past twenty years.[11] "Studies show that 13-year-olds who sniff fumes to get high are more likely to grow into 15-year-old chronic abusers of illicit drugs," according to Herb Kleber, M.D., medical director of the Center on Addiction and Substance Abuse at Columbia.[12]

Experts say that there are clear signs that the effects of drug education have worn off. Having watched fewer cautionary filmstrips and heard fewer of the firsthand horror stories that shook up previous generations, the youngest teenagers are feeling as if they cannot be harmed by drugs.[13]

Research has shown a high connection between individuals' drug use and that of their friends.

- *A person with friends who use a drug will be more likely to try the drug.*

- *The individual who is already using a drug will be likely to introduce friends to the experience.*

- *Users are more likely to establish friendships with others who are users already.*[14]

Experts have noted that physical access to illegal drugs and peer pressure probably contribute to the change in patterns of use.

Adults

Christopher Louis Gonzales lost his wife to a ninety-eight-cent can of gold spray paint. His twenty-eight-year-old wife died in his arms as they sat on their sofa. "Paint, it had a lot to do with it," he said. The autopsy report confirmed that paint inhalation contributed to her death. Their four children were placed with their grandmother in another state.

Gonzales is addicted to sniffing paint. He said he would like to stop, but it is too easy to slip back. "It's like climbing a mountain. You're climbing and you're way up there and you fall back, and then you start to climb again."[15]

Most studies on the subject of inhalant abuse focus on adolescents. Adults at risk for solvent abuse include those whose work brings them into contact with these substances. Few attempts have been made to identify the prevalence of solvent abuse in industry.[16] Yet, painters, printers, hair stylists, custodial engineers and maintenance workers, gas station operators, workers in car repair shops or dry cleaning establishments, and those involved in the refinement of petroleum products or the manufacture of products containing solvents are among those exposed to organic solvents in occupational settings.[17]

Deprived of their drugs of choice, imprisoned substance abusers often abuse inhalants. This can occur in other isolated settings, as well. Medical workers over the last century have been at risk for abuse of ether, chloroform, and more recently halothane (an inhalation anesthetic)—with sometime fatal results.[18]

Profile of Sniffers

Research studies show that many inhalant users are unhappy. They seek escape and often fail to think in a realistic manner. Users may have the feeling that nothing can hurt them. Such feelings may cause foolish acts, resulting in danger to the user and others.

Inhalant abusers may feel that no one can tell them what to

do. These feelings of superiority may lead to aggressive or violent behavior. Individuals who have been abused or neglected by their parents may have good reason to want to forget their problems—and inhalants provide that escape. Living in such an environment often hampers a child's emotional growth.

One study conducted in a southwestern city in the United States found that inhalant-using delinquents, in comparison to other delinquents, had been arrested almost three times more frequently, were arrested more often for more serious crimes, and were younger at the time they were first arrested.[19]

Inhalant users tend to have a small, close group of friends who act very differently from other people of society.[20] Young people who sniff have an overwhelming desire to belong. The most striking example of peer influence on inhalant use appeared in a study of street children in Mexico City. Kids in these street gangs came from poor families. The group of gang members functioned as a substitute family with no punishment for use of drugs.[21]

How Can You Tell if Someone Is Using Inhalants?

There is no simple way to identify inhalant abusers. However, if you suspect someone you know is sniffing solvents, aerosols, or similar substances, the following telltale signs may indicate involvement with substance abuse:

- *Drunken appearance—slurred speech, rowdy behavior, loss of coordination, bloodshot eyes—without the smell of alcohol*
- *Chemical smell on skin, breath, or clothing*

- *Paint residue on body or clothing*
- *Rash, spots, or sores around the mouth and nose*
- *Runny nose, cough, or other persistent flu-like symptoms*
- *Pysical deterioration—rapid weight loss, nausea, headaches, memory losses, or difficulty in concentration*
- *Less responsible behavior—decrease in interest or performance at work or school*
- *Sudden lack of interest in former activities, sports, or friends*
- *Drowsiness or confusion*
- *Keeping aerosols, solvent containers, plastic bags, or similar products in the bathroom or bedroom*[22]

A Teen's Real-life Story

Emily* is seventeen. Behind the piercing eyes, shaking hands, and effortless smile is Emily's story.

"One day, while painting my fingernails, I discovered I really loved the smell and the woozy effect it had on me. I was thirteen years old and in the seventh-grade. I knew my Dad did paint and the bag stuff when he was my age. I was not going to be like my dad. But I turned out to be just like him."

Emily admits to smoking marijuana once or twice and occasionally drinking alcoholic beverages.

"I put up a good front when I was home. If I wasn't sober, I managed to look and act sober. In school, I would brush clear

---

* Not her real name.

nail polish in the palm of my hand and go to sleep. I even borrowed Wite-Out™ from the teacher's desk."

Emily goes to Narcotics Anonymous (NA) meetings regularly. She keeps in daily contact with her NA sponsor. She has been "clean" for about four months.

"I became aggressive when I went through withdrawals. I blacked out once. I still have headaches. I always shake. I forget things. I knew about the dangers of hard drugs—but never inhalants. I was in the eleventh-grade when I first learned that this stuff can kill you."

Emily has been accepted by the Navy upon completion of high school. After her term in the Navy, her dream is to go into law enforcement.[23]

Questions for Discussion

1. How do you think peer pressure influences inhalant abuse?

2. Are inhalants included in your drug education classes? If not, what could you do to get them added?

3. How can you identify someone who is using inhalants?

7
Treatment and Prevention

One of the problems with treating inhalant abuse is the difficulty of providing the long-term care that is needed. Many drug treatment facilities refuse to treat the inhalant abuser. Traditionally, inhalant abusers are difficult to treat.[1] Compared to other forms of drug abuse, huffers and sniffers exhibit high rates of treatment failure and relapse.

Treatment of the Inhalant Abuser

Inhalant abusers are among the most difficult to treat. Research shows that inhalant users have serious social and personal problems. Most drug rehabilitation programs cannot handle these types of problems.[2] Many treatment programs for chronic inhalant abusers are only four weeks in length. Since chronic abusers suffer the effects of inhalants for months after they stop, inhalant abusers are often still "under the influence" when treatment ends.

Many professionals believe that longer treatment efforts with specific programs and approaches are needed to address the complex psychosocial, economic, and biophysical issues of the inhalant abuser. When brain injury is present, the treatment becomes slower and more difficult.[3]

In general, there is a prolonged period of freeing the body of dependence or addiction to a substance and recovery of nerve function, as well as many other problems. Because of this, inhalant abusers need to be treated in separate programs.[4] The lack of knowledge about treatment issues is widespread.

Treatment for inhalant abusers should include:

- *Early intervention*
- *Adequate detoxification time*
- *Comprehensive assessment and programming*[5]

A Model Treatment Program

At the beginning of the 1990s, one field expert noted that "treatment facilities set up for inhalant abusers are nonexistent." Another expressed concern over the "lack of even a rudimentary model."[6]

In an attempt to fill this void, Our Home, Inc., in Huron, South Dakota, received a grant in 1991 from the U.S. Department of Health and Human Services—Center for Substance Abuse

Treatment to develop an inhalant abuse treatment model. The demonstration project was funded to implement specialized services for youth with inhalant abuse problems.[7] The innovative programming of Our Home, Inc., Inhalant Abuse Treatment Program is considered to be one of the most comprehensive in the world.

Due to project funding requirements, 85 percent of the patients at the sixteen-bed residential facility are Native American adolescents from South Dakota. In addition, it has served a limited number of inhalant-abusing youth from all across the country, including Vermont, Alaska, Montana, Michigan, Florida, and Oregon.

Our Home, Inc., provides an extended length of stay, allowing a minimum patient stay of 90 days with extension capacity to 120 days. The average patient age at admission 13.2 years, and the average age of first use has been 10.2 years. Many of these children had no prior knowledge about the dangers of using inhalants. A typical patient has used inhalants for about three years before entering treatment. By April 1995 more than one hundred patients had been treated, 73 percent of them male.[8]

Steve Reidel, associate director of Our Home, Inc., said, "Our patients admit to having abused five or six chemicals. The kids have told us that their drugs of choice include gasoline, rubber cement, spray paint, and correction fluid. Eighty-six percent of the youth report unsuccessful efforts to stop using inhalants."[9]

Increasing evidence suggests that people affected by this problem can be identified and successfully treated, but early intervention appears to be critical. Our Home, Inc., indicates that there is cause for concern, but also for hope of recovery.[10]

Prevention

Nationally, inhalant abuse continues to rise as more and more children, many of them not yet in their teens, embark on a destructive journey, unaware of the pitfalls that lie ahead. Hundreds die from inhalant abuse each year. Unfortunately, many adults remain ignorant of this growing problem, often referred to as the "silent epidemic." Choosing appropriate and effective prevention efforts is one of the most difficult problems in the inhalant abuse field.[11]

What Can Be Done About Inhalant Abuse?

Awareness and education are two of the keys to combating inhalant abuse. The adult population must recognize inhalant abuse for the serious danger it presents to health and society and realize that what was once perceived to be a problem affecting only the poor and neglected is becoming increasingly common among middle-class and upper-middle-class youth. Awareness is just beginning to develop. In 1994, the Parent Teacher Association (PTA) became the first national education and parent organization to officially recognize and address the problem of inhalant abuse throughout its membership. (PTA membership consists of almost 7 million people throughout the world.)[12] Also, the American Bar Association adopted a resolution in August 1995, recognizing inhalant abuse as a problem.

Strong programs, focusing on the recognition and treatment of solvent abuse, need to be developed in order to convey accurate and preventive information to youth, their parents, school personnel, criminal justice and health care professionals,

SNIFFING CORRECTION FLUID CAN STOP YOUR HEART.

If you sniff to get high, you are inhaling poisons that do definite damage. So stop—before your heart does.

and community and government agencies. The media can also play a critical role in the education process.

The First Line of Defense—Education

"I started using inhalants in the seventh grade, but my mother didn't know about it until last year," said a high school senior. "And then the school told her."[13]

A member of the Concord High wrestling team in Concord, New Hampshire, described the experience of using inhalants in the following way: "You see a blinking red light and you hear auditory hallucinations—stuff that doesn't make sense. Then the blinking gets really fast and you pass out." He ran into a wall when he passed out but still thought the experience was exciting.

The wrestler said he had never been caught using drugs and had no criminal record. He insisted his parents had no idea he used inhalants and other mind-altering substances. His clean-cut image and his innocent smile help hide his habits.[14]

Julie Lange of Long Valley, New Jersey, lost her son Justin, sixteen years old, after he inhaled nitrous oxide with a trash bag over his head. He was in a coma for three days before he was pronounced brain dead. "I thought I knew the signs and symptoms of drug abuse, but I knew nothing about inhalant abuse," his mother said.[15]

Ralph Engel, president of Chemical Specialties Manufacturers Association, said, "Most products manufactured have bold labeling."[16] Unfortunately, this has not kept people from using products in ways that were never intended.

One of the most effective ways to fight inhalant abuse is to educate parents, teachers, and young people about the dangers of many commonly used products and the warning signs of abuse.

Inhalants

Teachers and parents need to be made aware of research findings and available resources, and encouraged to participate in training programs designed to combat inhalant abuse.

Adults can educate children about the dangers and the responsible use of legal products with the potential for inhalant abuse. Children's use of these products needs to be supervised.[17]

Experts contend that, starting at the lower grades, the warning should not emphasize drug abuse, but begin with the caution that "strong smells should be avoided."

"With the little guys," said Fred Beauvais, a research scientist, "we want to avoid suggestions of drugs and say it is poison avoidance when it comes to inhalants."[18]

Despite the serious consequences of inhalant abuse, Dr. Charles Sharp, administrator for the National Institute on Drug Abuse, said that antidrug educators are afraid to talk to teens about inhalant abuse because "they are under the wrong belief that if they say anything, kids will start it because inhalants are so widely available." Yet statistics show that many children already have learned about inhalants from their peers, so educators would not be the first to let them know about inhalants.[19]

Teaching decision-making skills, including refusal strategies, must be part of any effective prevention strategy, starting as young as three years of age. It is essential that children be equipped with motivation, self-esteem, and the tools to resist peer pressure. Children need to be made aware of the consequences of the use of these substances in honest and factual terms.[20]

What can schools do?

- *Monitor students' access to abusable substances in the school setting.*

Parents need to develop good communication with their children and inform them of the health consequences of substance abuse.

- *Share information about the hazards of inhalant abuse with colleagues.*
- *Be alert to signs of inhalant abuse by students.*
- *Incorporate information about inhalant abuse in drug prevention curricula.*
- *Inform parents of the hazards, signs, and symptoms of inhalant abuse.*
- *Identify appropriate intervention and referral services for abusers.*
- *Encourage the development of student support groups for those who may need them.*[21]

Communities

Community involvement is key to solving the problem of inhalant abuse. This requires a well-educated public and commitment to change. Communities need to develop and carry out innovative ways to prevent inhalant abuse. For substance abuse prevention to be effective, it must actively engage as many segments of the community as possible. Factual and reliable information and materials must be made available. In order to reach the widest audience, the media must be an active partner in spreading the information.[22]

The Texas Prevention Partnership, which founded and leads the National Inhalant Prevention Coalition, is a semiprivate organization formed in response to spiraling drug abuse in that state. This organization promotes a national campaign that outlines the dangers of aerosol sprays, cigarette lighters, and other household products. According to Harvey Weiss, executive director of the Texas Prevention Partnership, the Inhalants &

Poisons Awareness Week they initiated in 1993 promotes education and awareness as the best and most effective ways to reduce and eliminate inhalant abuse. The Texas Prevention Partnership provides materials on how to conduct a local awareness and media campaign to community coordinators.[23]

More than one thousand organizations from forty-five states joined the campaign in 1995 in an effort to mount effective community-based campaigns and expand local involvement. This annual campaign, held the third week in March, has become a model in the fight against inhalant abuse.

National surveys conducted in 1994 reported that the use of inhalants continued to rise. Following two years of aggressive inhalant prevention campaigning in Texas, the 1994 state survey of more than one hundred seventy thousand Texas students showed 20 percent of seventh graders had tried inhalants, decreasing from 25.9 percent in 1992. Overall, there has been a 19.5 percent decrease among high school students and a 39 percent decrease in inhalant use among elementary school students.[24]

The Partnership for a Drug-Free America, a volunteer organization of communications companies, launched an education campaign in 1995 to alert the public to the dangers of inhaling chemicals. The program entails distribution of a series of print and television warning ads to the nation's forty largest media markets. "We want to let teens know that inhaling things to get high can kill you," said Richard D. Bonnette, president of the partnership.[25]

Manufacturers have tried putting additives, such as foul-smelling or irritating substances, in abused products. Additives and restrictions on sales are well intended, but they have not worked. Warnings on labels have virtually been ignored by the inhalant user. Present-day laws regarding abuse of inhalants are ineffective because each inhalant has a legitimate use, making it difficult to police the misuse of these chemicals. However some states and communities have laws, ordinances, or both prohibiting the sale of certain products to minors. Education may well be the only weapon against inhalant abuse.[26]

If you know someone who needs help, seek assistance from:

- *Family and friends.*
- *Teachers and counselors.*
- *Hot lines and referral services.*
- *Drug treatment programs.*
- *Drug abuse counselors.*
- *Mental health agencies.*
- *Your physician or other health professional.*
- *Organizations in your area. Check the yellow pages under "Drug Abuse."*
- *Chemical dependency programs.*
- *Alateen, an organization of Al-Anon for teenage friends and family members of abusers. This group has chapters in cities across the United States.*

Given the growing body of evidence about the hazards of inhalant abuse, its impact, and its consequences, the time has come to move beyond slogans, catchwords, and glib phrases. Information must replace slogans, and knowledge must replace ignorance about the dangers of inhalants. The challenge is to deter experimentation and to interrupt patterns of use. To combat this form of abuse, every effort must be made to provide strong anti-inhalant education, prevention, treatment, and recovery programs, carefully designed to stop this waste of human potential.

Questions for Discussion

1. Investigate what your local community is doing to prevent inhalant abuse. Could more be done? How?

2. What problems are associated with the treatment of inhalant abusers?

3. Some people believe that educating youth about inhalants increases the risk of use. What do you think?

Where to Go for Help

For more information on inhalant abuse contact:

Alateen
P.O. Box 862
Midtown Station
New York, NY 10018-0862
(212) 302-7240

International Institute for Inhalant Abuse
450 W. Jefferson Ave.
Englewood, CO 80110
(303) 788-1951

National Inhalant Prevention Coalition
1305 Lorrain St.
#A
Austin, TX 78703
(512) 480-8953

National Institute on Drug Abuse
5600 Fishers Lane
Room 9A53
Rockville, MD 20857
(301) 443-1514

Our Home, Inc.
360 Ohio SW
Huron, SD 57350
(605) 352-4368

Partnership For a Drug-Free America
405 Lexington Ave., 16th Floor
New York, NY 10174
(212) 922-1560

Chapter Notes

Chapter 1

1. Alan Vanneman, "Inhalants: The Orphans of Drug Abuse," *Youth Today*, November/December 1993, p. 23.

2. Tanya Bricking, "Study: Teens 'Huff' Inhalants for High," *Cincinnati Enquirer*, July 18, 1993, News Bank HEA 75:E9.

3. Renee Ordway, "Inhalants Become 'Drug of Choice' in Schools, Abuse Specialists Say," *Bangor Daily News*, April 3, 1993, News Bank HEA 37:E1.

4. Shari Roan, "Cheap Thrill Can Become a Deadly High," *Los Angeles Times*, vol. 112, April 27, 1993, pp. B10, B11.

5. Sidney Cohen, "Inhalant Abuse: An Overview of the Problem," in *Review of Inhalants: Euphoria to Dysfunction*, Research Monograph 15 (Rockville, Md.: National Institute on Drug Abuse, 1977), p. 2.

6. Edward M. Bercher, *Licit and Illicit Drugs* (Boston: Little Brown and Company, 1972), p. 311.

7. Andrea Kaminski, *Mind-Altering Drugs: Inhalants* (Madison, Wis.: Wisconsin Clearinghouse, 1991), p. 8.

8. John R. Glowa, *Inhalants* (New York: Chelsea House, 1992), p. 29.

9. Ibid, pp. 30–31.

10. Bercher, p. 316.

11. Lowell Showalter, "Inhalation of Volatile Substances," *Inhalants* (Tempe, Ariz.: Do It Now Foundation Publications, 1993), p. 2.

12. Bercher, p. 317.

13. Charles W. Sharp, "Introduction to Inhalant Abuse," in *Inhalant Abuse: Volatile Research Agenda*, Research Monograph 129 (Rockville, Md.: National Institute on Drug Abuse, 1992), p. 2.

14. Glowa, p. 32.

15. Cohen, p. 3.

16. "Drug Use Among Pre-High School Children Rising," *Greenville News*, December 13, 1994, p.13A.

17. Richard Scatterday, "How Physicians Can Help to Clear the Air Regarding Inhalant Abuse," Fact Sheet, Austin, Tex.: Texas Prevention Partnership, 1994.

18. David Holmstrom, "Use of Drugs among Teenagers Starts With Sniffing Common Home Chemicals," *The Christian Science Monitor*, May 10, 1994, p. 1.

19. Kristen Vaughn, "Inhalants Killing Hundreds of Teens," *Herald-Journal*, April 13, 1995, p. A3.

20. Earl Siegel and Susan Wason, "Sudden Death Following Inhalation of Butane and Propane: Changing Trends," *Inhalant Abuse: A Volatile Research Agenda*, Research Monograph 129 (Rockville, Md.: National Institute on Drug Abuse, 1992), p. 193.

Chapter 2

1. Jolene L. Roehikepartain, *Inhalants: Nasal Warfare* (Silver Spring, Md.: The Health Connection, 1990).

2. John R. Glowa, *Inhalants* (New York: Chelsea House, 1992), p. 37.

3. Mark Pownall, *Inhalants* (New York: Franklin Watts, 1987), p. 12.

4. "Study Shows Drug Use Among Teens Getting Worse," *Greenville Piedmont*, December 12, 1994, p. 1A.

5. Bob Trebilcock, "Fatal Attraction: How 'Huffing Kills,'" *Redbook*, March 1993, p. 120.

6. Charles W. Sharp and Neil Rosenberg, "Volatile Substances," *Substance Abuse: A Comprehensive Textbook*. eds. Joyce H Lowinson, et al. (Baltimore, Md.: Williams & Wilkins, 1992), p. 307.

7. *Inhalants*, pamphlet (Washington, D.C.: Department of Health, Education and Welfare, 1979).

8. Neil L. Rosenberg and Charles W. Sharp, "Solvent Toxicity: A Neurological Focus," *Inhalant Abuse: A Volatile Research Agenda*, Research Monograph 129 (Rockville, Md.: National Institute on Drug Abuse, 1992), p. 117.

9. R.J. Ignelzi, "Cheap, Easy Inhalants Are Killers," *San Diego Union Tribune*, June 6, 1992, p. 11.

10. Catherine O'Neill, "Fumes That Can Kill You," *Washington Post*, March 15, 1994, p. WH 18.

11. Ignelzi, p. 11.

12. Sharp and Rosenberg, p. 307.

13. Charles W. Sharp, "Introduction to Inhalant Abuse," *Inhalant Abuse: Volatile Research Agenda*, Research Monograph 129 (Rockville, Md.: National Institute on Drug Abuse, 1992), p. 8.

14. Andrea Kaminski, *Mind-Altering Drugs: Inhalants* (Madison, Wis: Wisconsin Clearinghouse, 1991), p. 6.

15. "Inhalant Abuse Fact Sheet," Austin, Tex.: Texas Prevention Partnership, 1995.

16. Pownall, p. 43.

17. Joseph Westermeyer, "The Psychiatrist and Solvent-Inhalant Abuse: Recognition, Assessment, and Treatment," *American Journal of Psychiatry*, July 1987, p. 905.

18. Ignelzi, p. 11.

Chapter 3

1. Cynthia Crossley, "Madisonville Teen Dies After Inhaling Aerosol," *The Courier-Journal*, November 7, 1991, p. 2.

2. Fred Beauvais, "Volatile Solvent Abuse: Trends and Patterns," in *Inhalant Abuse: A Volatile Research Agenda*, Research Monograph 129 (Rockville, Md.: National Institute on Drug Abuse, 1992), p. 14.

3. Mark Pownall, *Inhalants* (New York: Franklin Watts, 1987), p. 33.

4. Joe Kavac, "15-Year-Old Girl Dies After Inhaling Aerosol Spray Product," *Macon Telegraph*, March 1, 1992, p. 1A.

5. Bob Trebilcock, "Fatal Attraction: How Huffing Kills," *Redbook*, March 1993, p. 120.

6. Ann Schrader, "Commonly Abused Solvent Ravages Fatty Tissue in Brain, Nerves," *Denver Post*, September 23, 1990, *News Bank HEA* 103:C8.

7. Ibid.

8. Stephen Hunt and Anne Wilson, "Some Teens Using Dangerous Inhalants for 'High'," *Salt Lake City Tribune*, February 19, 1989, *News Bank* 19:D8.

9. Cara Neth, "Inhalants Attack Nervous System, Killing Sniffers," *Fort Collins Coloradoan*, January 10, 1988, *News Bank HEA* 5:B14.

10. Jolene L. Roehikepartain, *Inhalants: Nasal Warfare* (Silver Spring, Md.: The Health Connection, 1990).

11. David W. McDougall, "Mother Warns against Butane High," *The Post and Courier*, April 18, 1992, p. 1.

12. T.L. Stanley, "Teens Pay Big Price for Cheap Butane High," *Louisville Courier-Journal*, January 5, 1991, *News Bank HEA* 3:G8-3G9.

13. Ibid.

14. "Student Suffered Butane Poisoning," *Greenville Piedmont*, January 18, 1995, p. 2C.

15. Melinda Gladfelter, "Statistics Show Inhalants Popular Among Teen-Agers," *Greenville Piedmont*, January 27, 1993, p. 1A.

16. Automotive Service Excellence, *Refrigerant Recovery and Recycling*, booklet (Washington, D.C.: Automotive Service Excellence, 1991), pp. 1–2.

17. Dale Huffman, "Mother Mourns Loss with Message: Sniffing Chemicals Snuffs Out Lives," *Dayton Daily News*, October 30, 1991, pp. 1A, 10A.

18. Jim Hutton, "Freon," *San Antonio Express News*, May 20, 1990, *News Bank HEA* 50:D6.

19. Hunt and Wilson, 19:D8.

20. Laura Sessions Stepp, "Sniffing Fumes: the Two-Minute High That Can Last a Lifetime," *Washington Post*, January 30, 1994, p. A1.

21. Gilda Berger, *Addiction* (New York: Franklin Watts, 1992), p. 101.

22. Andrea Kaminski, *Mind-Altering Drugs: Inhalants* (Madison, Wis.: Wisconsin Clearinghouse, 1991), p 5.

23. John R. Glowa, *Inhalants*, (New York: Chelsea House, 1992), p. 72.

24. "Clearing the Air on Inhalants," *Health Safety Update*, The National PTA, January 1994.

25. Earl Siegel and Suman Wason, "Sudden Sniffing Death Following Inhalation of Butane and Propane: Changing Trends," in *Inhalant Abuse: Volatile Research Agenda*, Research Monograph 129 (Rockville, Md.: National Institute on Drug Abuse, 1992), p. 194.

26. "Inhalant Abuse and Sudden Sniffing Death," Cincinnati, Ohio.: Cincinnati Drug & Poison Information Center, information sheet, undated.

27. Siegel and Wason, p. 196.

28. McDougall, p. 1.

Chapter 4

1. Roger P. Maickel, "The Fate and Toxicity of Butyl Nitrites," in *Health Hazards of Nitrite Inhalants*, Research Monograph 83, eds. Harry W. Haverkos and John Dougherty (Rockville, Md.: National Institute on Drug Abuse, 1988), p. 2.

2. Charles W. Sharp and Neil L. Rosenberg, "Volatile Substances," in *Substance Abuse: A Comprehensive Textbook*, eds. Joyce H. Lowinson, et al. (Baltimore, Md.: Williams & Wilkins, 1992), p. 318.

3. *Inhalants*, pamphlet (Northfield, Minn.: Life Skills Education, 1994), p. 2.

4. W. Robert Lange, et al., "Nitrite Inhalants: Contemporary Patterns of Abuse," in *Health Hazards of Nitrite Inhalants*, Research Monograph 83, eds. Harry W. Haverkos and John Dougherty (Rockville, Md: National Institute on Drug Abuse, 1988), p. 86.

5. Guy R. Newell, et al., "Nitrite Inhalants: Historical Perspective," in *Health Hazards of Nitrite Inhalants*, eds. Harry W. Haverkos and John Dougherty, Research Monograph 83 (Rockville, Md.: National Institute on Drug Abuse, 1988), p. 2.

6. Ibid., p. 6.

7. Clifford Sherry, *Inhalants* (New York: The Rosen Publishing Group, Inc. 1994), p. 21.

8. Newell, p. 4.

9. Reginald G. Smart, "Inhalant Abuse in Canada," *Epidemiology of Inhalant Abuse: An Update*, eds. Raquel A. Crider and Beatrice A. Rouse, Research Monograph 85 (Rockville, Md.: National Institute on Drug Abuse, 1988), p. 122.

10. Jack Douglas, "Potentially Lethal Aerosol Sprays Gaining Popularity as Legal Highs," *Houston Post*, February 27, 1989, *News Bank HEA* 19:D6.

11. W.R. Spence, *Inhalants: The Quick, Deadly High*, booklet, (Waco, Tex.: Health Edco, 1992), p. 6.

12. Ibid.

13. Christine Dye, *Amyl/Butyl Nitrite & Nitrous Oxide*, pamphlet, (Tempe, Ariz.: Do It Now Foundation, 1990).

14. Andrea Kaminski, *Mind-Altering Drugs: Inhalants* (Madison, WI: Wisconsin Clearinghouse, 1991), p 7.

15. Mark Lisheron, "No Laughing Matter: Inhaling Gas Brings a Risky Thrill," *Milwaukee Journal*, September 14, 1988, *News Bank HEA* 115:F5.

16. Karen Goldberg, "Teens Get High From Whip-its," *Washington Times*, February 4, 1993, *News Bank HEA* 12:D1.

17. Peter Pae, "Sobering Side of Laughing Gas," *Washington Post*, September 16, 1994, p. B4.

18. Ericka Pizillo,"Laughing Gas Is Not For Laughs," *Akron Beacon Journal*, October 23, 1993, *News Bank* HEA 104: F8.

19. Pae, p. B4.

20. Dye, pamphlet.

Chapter 5

1. Alan Vanneman, "Inhalants: The Orphans of Drug Abuse," *Youth Today*, November/December 1993, p. 23.

2. Phil Galewitz, "Inhalant Abuse Lethal, and Rising," *Patriot News*, February 17, 1991, *News Bank HEA* 12:G8.

3. Leslie Sowers, "I Knew It Killed Brain Cells Big Time," *Houston Chronicle*, July 22, 1990, *News Bank HEA* 76:B14.

4. Author phone interview with Harvey Weiss, January 12, 1995.

5. *Inhalants: The Silent Epidemic*, Discussion Leader's Guide, (Austin, Tex.: Texas Prevention Partnership, 1992), pp. 7–8.

6. Sowers, 76: B12-B13.

7. *Inhalants: The Silent Epidemic*, booklet (Austin, Tex.: Texas Prevention Partnership, 1994).

8. Mark Pownall, *Inhalants* (New York: Franklin Watts, 1987), pp. 8, 10

9. E.R. Oetting and Jay Webb, "Psychosocial Characteristics and Their Links With Inhalants: A Research Agenda," in *Inhalant Abuse: A Volatile Research Agenda*, eds. Charles Sharpe, et al., Research Monograph 129 (Rockville, Md.: National Institute on Drug Abuse, 1992), pp. 60–62.

10. Brigid O'Malley, "Huffing: A High That's Cheap, Easy—and Deadly," *Naples Daily News*, June 27, 1993, *News Bank HEA* 75:E8.

11. Charles W. Sharp and Neil L. Rosenberg, "Volatile Substances," *Substance Abuse: A Comprehensive Textbook*, eds. Joyce H. Lowinson, et al. (Baltimore, Md.: Williams & Wilkins, 1992), p. 305.

12. Shari Roan, "Cheap Thrill Can Become a Deadly High," *Los Angeles Times*, April 27, 1993, p. B10.

13. Ibid., B11.

14. Author phone interview with Jane Chittick, March 6, 1995.

15. Shirley Downing, "Mom's Loss Grief Compel her to Warn of Huffing," *The Commercial Appeal*, February 27, 1992, p. B1.

16. "Parents Should Be Alert to Signs of Inhalant Abuse," Ann Landers column, *Greenville Piedmont*, March 24, 1995, p. 5 B.

17. Karen Goldberg, "Teens Get High From 'Whip-its'," *Washington Times*, February 4, 1993, *News Bank HEA* 12:D1.

18. Sowers, 76:B14.

19. Richard Scatterday, "How Physicians Can Help to Clear the Air Regarding Inhalant Abuse," Fact Sheet, Austin, Tex.: Texas Prevention Partnership, 1994.

20. W.R. Spence, *Inhalants: The Quickly, Deadly High* (Waco, Tex.: Health Edco, 1992), p. 3

21. David J. Wilmes, Director of Training and Consultation at the Johnson Institute in Minneapolis, Minn., spoke on the topic, "Parenting For Prevention," Lowcountry Parent Summit, The Citadel's McAlister Field House, Charleston, S.C., March 25, 1995.

22. Gilda Berger, *Addiction* (New York: Franklin Watts, 1992), pp. 21–22.

23. O'Malley, 75:E8.

24. Christine N. Brown, "The Rising Use of Drugs By Teens," *Good Housekeeping*, April 1994, p. 191.

25. Pierre Thomas, "Illicit Drug Use Rises Among U.S. Teenagers," *Washington Post*, February 1, 1994, *News Bank HEA* 7:G6.

26. Lloyd D. Johnson, *1994 Results of the Monitoring the Future Study*, Press Release, Washington, D.C., December 12, 1994.

Chapter 6

1. *Inhalants: The Silent Epidemic*, booklet, Austin, Tex.: Texas Prevention Partnership, 1995, p. 2.

2. "A Global Problem," *Adolescence*, September 1993, p. 47.

3. Sidney Cohen, "Inhalant Abuse: An Overview of the Problem," in *Review of Inhalants: Euphoria to Dysfunction*, eds. Charles W. Sharp and Mary Lee Brehm, Research Monograph 15 (Rockville, Md.: National Institute on Drug Abuse 1977), p. 4.

4. W.R. Spence, *Inhalants: The Quick, Deadly High* (Waco, Tex.: Health Edco, 1992), p. 13.

5. Diana Williams, "Inhalant Highs Can Offer Lethal Lows," *Kansas City Star*, July 23, 1990, *News Bank HEA* 76:B10.

6. Alan Vanneman, "Inhalants: The Orphans of Drug Abuse," *Youth Today*, November/December 1993, p. 23.

7. *Inhalants*, pamphlet (Northfield, Minn.: Life Skills Education, 1994), p. 11.

8. Mark Brunswick, "More Pre-teens Becoming Abusers of Cheap Inhalants," *Minneapolis Star Tribune*, March 26, 1989, p. A1.

9. Vanneman, p. 23.

10. "Study Shows Drug Use Among Teens Getting Worse," *Greenville Piedmont*, December 12, 1994, p. 1A.

11. Fred Beauvais, "Volatile Solvent Abuse: Trends and Patterns," in *Inhalant Abuse: A Volatile Research Agenda*, eds. Charles Sharpe, et al., Research Monograph 129 (Rockville, Md.: National Institute on Drug Abuse, 1992), p. 22.

12. Linda Bernstein, "Drugs in the '90s," *McCall's*, April 1995, p. 120.

13. "A New Generation, an Old Danger," *Reader's Digest*, June 1994, p. 146.

14. *National Survey Results on Drug Use From The Monitoring The Future Study, 1975-1993* (Rockville, Md.: National Institute on Drug Abuse, 1994), p. 228.

15. Ann Scrader and Alan Gottlieb, "Solvent Sniffing: Deadly and Growing," *Denver Post*, September 23, 1990, *News Bank HEA* 103:C2.

16. Charles W. Sharp and Neil L. Rosenberg, "Volatile Substances," *Substance Abuse: A Comprehensive Textbook*, eds. Joyce H. Lowinson, et al. (Baltimore, Md.: Williams & Wilkins, 1992) p. 310.

17. Joseph Westermeyer, "The Psychiatrist And Solvent-Inhalant Abuse: Recognition, Assessment, and Treatment," *American Journal of Psychiatry*, July 1987, p. 904.

18. Ibid.

19. E.R. Oetting and Jay Webb, "Psychological Characteristics and Their Links With Inhalants: A Research Agenda," *Inhalant Abuse: A Volatile Research Agenda*, eds. Charles Sharpe, et al., Research Monograph 129 (Rockville, Md.: National Institute on Drug Abuse, 1992), p. 64.

20. Oetting and Webb, p. 67.

21. E.R. Oetting and et. al, in "Social and Psychological Factors Underlying Inhalant Abuse," *Epidemiology of Inhalant Abuse: An Update*, eds. Raquel A. Crider and Beatrice A. Rouse, Monograph Series No. 85 (Rockville, Md.: National Institute on Drug Abuse, 1988), p. 183.

22. American Council for Drug Education, *The Challenge: Focus on Inhalants*, Washington, D.C.: Department of Education, vol. 5, no. 4, p. 3.

23. Author interview, Greenville, S.C., January 10, 1995.

Chapter 7

1. Neil L. Rosenberg and Charles W. Sharp, "Solvent Toxicity: A Neurological Focus," in *Inhalant Abuse: A Volatile Research Agenda*, eds. Charles Sharp, et al., Research Monograph 129 (Rockville, Md.: National Institute on Drug Abuse, 1992), p. 121.

2. Pamela Jumper-Thurman and Fred Beauvais, "Treatment of Volatile Solvent Abusers," in *Inhalant Abuse: A Volatile Research Agenda*, Research Monograph 129, eds. Charles Sharp, et al. (Rockville, Md.: National Institute on Drug Abuse, 1992), p. 203.

3. Rosenberg and Sharp, p. 121.

4. Jumper-Thurman and Beauvais, p. 210.

5. Steve Riedel, "A Breath of Death," *Adolescence*, September 1993, p. 51.

6. Jumper-Thurman and Beauvais, p. 203.

7. Steve Riedel, "Inhalants: A Growing Health Concern," *Behavioral Health Management Magazine*, May/June 1995, p.28.

8. Author phone interview with Steve Riedel, March 23, 1995.

9. Ibid.

10. Riedel, "Inhalants: A Growing Health Concern," p. 28.

11. *Understanding Inhalant Users*, booklet (Austin, Tex.: Texas Commission on Alcohol and Drug Abuse, 1991), p. 28.

12. *Viewpoint*, newsletter (Austin, Tex.: Texas Prevention Partnership, Summer 1994), p. 4.

13. Author interview with anonymous high school senior, Greenville, S.C., January 9, 1995.

14. Anmarie Timmins, "Inhalants Offer Students a Deadly High," *Concord Monitor*, May 4, 1994, *News Bank HEA* 28:F9-10.

15. "New Campaign Warns About Dangers of Teen Inhalant Abuse," *Greenville Piedmont*, April 14, 1995, p. 3A.

16. Ibid.

17. The National PTA, *Health Safety Update*, "Clearing the Air on Inhalant Abuse," January 1994.

18. David Holmstrom, "Use of Drugs Among Teenagers Starts with Sniffing Common Home Chemicals," *The Christian Science Monitor*, May 10, 1994, p. 4.

19. Melinda Gladfelter, "A Drug Problem Ignored: Statistics Show Inhalants Popular Among Teen-Agers," *Greenville Piedmont*, January 27, 1993, p. 8A.

20. Harvey J. Weiss, *Inhalants: The Silent Epidemic*, booklet (Austin: Tex., Texas Prevention Partnership, 1995), p. 3.

21. Richard C. Scatterday, "Inhalant Abuse," *The Challenge*, booklet (Washington, D.C.: U.S. Department of Education, 1994), vol. 5, no. 4, p. 4.

22. Weiss, p. 3.

23. Author phone interview with Harvey Weiss, January 12, 1995.

24. Harvey J. Weiss, "Inhalants: The Silent Epidemic," Lowcountry Parent Summit, The Citadel's McAlister Field House, Charleston, S.C., March 25, 1995.

25. Kristen Vaughan, "Inhalants Killing Hundreds of Teens," *Spartanburg Herald-Journal*, April 13, 1995, p. A3.

26. Karen Kerner, "Current Topics in Inhalant Abuse," in *Epidemology of Inhalant Abuse: An Update*, eds. Raquel A. Crider and Beatrice A. Rouse, Monograph Series no. 85 (Rockville, Md.: National Institute on Drug Abuse, 1988, pp. 20–21.

Glossary

Acquired Immunodeficiency Syndrome (AIDS)—A deadly disorder of the immune system of unknown cause that diminishes the body's resistance to certain infectious organisms.

addict—A person who is dependent on a drug.

asphyxiate—To kill or make unconscious by inadequate oxygen.

atrophy—A decrease in size or wasting away of a body part or tissue.

carcinogen—A substance that tends to cause cancer.

chlorofluorocarbon (CFC)—Any of several gaseous compounds that are used as refrigerants, cleaning solvents, and aerosol propellants.

chloroform—A heavy, colorless liquid hydrocarbon used chiefly in medicine as an anesthetic.

detoxification—Freeing the body of an addictive substance.

ether—An organic compound composed of oxygen, carbon, and hydrogen used to produce anesthesia.

euphoria—A feeling of well-being.

Fetal Solvent Syndrome—Physical malformations or mental defects that studies link to prenatal solvent abuse.

fluorocarbon—Any of various chemically inert compounds containing carbon and fluorine.

Freon™—Belongs to the class of chemicals called chlorofluorocarbons that contribute to the deletion of the ozone layer. Used as a refrigerant and as a propellant for aerosols.

hallucination—A sensory experience that does not exist outside the mind.

halothane—An inhalation anesthetic.

huffing—Soaking a rag with an inhalant, putting the rag over the mouth and nose, and inhaling. Also the street word for any kind of inhaling.

Human Immunodeficiency Virus (HIV)—The virus that is believed to cause AIDS.

Kaposi's sarcoma—A form of cancer associated with AIDS.

locker room—Street name for butyl nitrite.

nitrous oxide—A gas used in dentistry as an anesthetic and as a propellant in aerosol cans.

poppers—Street name for amyl nitrite.

sniffing—Breathing in an inhalant directly from the container.

solvent—A liquid substance capable of dissolving or dispersing one or more other substances to form a solution.

Sudden Sniffing Death (SSD)—Inhalation of some substances results in sudden death. It can happen with first-time use or after years of abuse.

tolerance—A decrease in the body's responsiveness to a drug due to repeated use, resulting in the user's need to increase the dosage in order to achieve the effects experienced previously.

toluene—A liquid aromatic hydrocarbon, which is a volatile solvent used in many industrial products such as glues, paints, and thinners, and is often abused as an inhalant.

volatile—Characterized by the tendency to rapidly change from a liquid to a vapor.

withdrawal—Stopping the regular use of a substance. Withdrawal symptoms can be psychological or physical.

Whippets™—Brand name for small cartridges of nitrous oxide.

Further Reading

The Challenge: Focus on Inhalants. Washington, D.C.: U.S. Department of Education, vol. 5, no. 4.

Epidemiology of Inhalant Abuse: An Update. Rockville, Md.: National Institute on Drug Abuse, Monograph Series, no. 85, 1990.

Glowa, John R. *Inhalants.* New York: Chelsea House, 1992.

Health Hazards of Nitrite Inhalants. Rockville, Md.: National Institute on Drug Abuse, Monograph Series, no. 83, 1990.

Inhalant Abuse: A Volatile Research Agenda. Rockville, Md.: National Institute on Drug Abuse, Monograph Series, no. 129, 1992.

Inhalant Abuse: Its Dangers Are Nothing to Sniff At. Rockville, Md.: National Institute on Drug Abuse, no. 94-3818, 1994.

Pownall, Mark. *Inhalants.* New York: Franklin Watts, 1987.

Synder, Solomon H. *Drugs and the Brain.* New York: Scientific American Books, 1986.

Understanding Inhalant Users. Austin, Tex.: Texas Commission on Alcohol and Drug Abuse, 1991.

Index

A
Acquired Immunodeficiency Syndrome (AIDS), 50, 52
aerosols
  abuse of, 30-33, 35-36, 38-39
  chemicals in, 31
  dangers of, 42-43
  definition of, 14, 30
  effects of, 39, 41-43
  patterns of use, 32
Alanon, 90
American Bar Association, 83
amyl nitrite
  definition of, 13, 45-46
  effects of, 48, 50
  medical use of, 48
  recreational use of, 48
anesthetic, 9, 11, 13, 20, 52, 75
arrhythmia, 26, 32

B
benzene, 24, 28
butane, 31, 33, 35, 36, 39, 60, 70
buytl nitrite
  definition of, 13, 45-46
  effects of, 50
  legal classification of, 48-49
  street names, 49

C
carcinogens, 24
chlorofluorocarbons (CFCs), 31, 36
chloroform, 7, 11, 75
Coleridge, Samuel, 7

D
Davy, Sir Humphry, 7
Delphi, 6
Drug Abuse Resistance Education (DARE), 63

E
ether, 7, 8, 9
euphoria, 17, 39

F
Fetal Solvent Syndrome, 24-55
fluorocarbons, 31, 39
Food and Drug Administration (FDA), 45-46, 48
Freon™ 31, 36, 38

G
gasoline, 11, 28, 70, 82
glue, 13, 20, 23, 25, 58, 60, 69-70

H
hallucinations, 23, 26, 39, 85
hallucinogenic substances, 6
halothane, 75
Holmes, Oliver Wendell, 9
huffing, 6, 18, 24

I
inhalants, *See also*: amyl nitrite, aerosols, butyl nitrite, nitrous oxide, solvents.
  definition of, 6
  religious use of, 6
  treatment, 13, 20, 80-83, 90-91
  trends, 64-65, 67, 72-74

111

International Institute for Inhalant Abuse, 21

J
Johnston, Lloyd D., 60, 67, 74

K
Kaposi's sarcoma, 52

L
Leshner, Alan I., 14

M
Monitoring the Future Study, 17, 60

N
National Inhalant Prevention Coalition, 57, 60, 67, 74
National Institute on Drug Abuse, 14, 25, 56, 63, 72, 86
n-hexane, 28
nitrites, 14, 45-46, 49, 50, 52
nitrous oxide
　abuse of, 7, 13, 52
　definition of, 14, 32, 52
　effects of, 52-54
　medical use of, 7, 9, 11, 52
　risks, 54, 85
　sources of, 52-54

O
Our Home, Inc., 81-83

P
paint thinner, 16, 58, 70
Parent Teacher Association (PTA), 83
Partnership for a Drug-Free America (PFDFA), 67, 89
"poppers", 46
prevention, 83, 85-86, 88-91
PRIDE, 72
Priestly, Sir Joseph, 7
propane, 31, 38, 39, 42

Q
Queen Victoria, 11

R
Riedel, Steve, 82
Roget, Peter, 7
Rosenberg, Neil, 21, 26, 32

S
Sharp, Charles, 56, 86
Simpson, James Y., 11
solvents
　absorption of, 20
　abuse of, 17, 20-21, 23, 28
　dangers of, 26-28
　elimination from the body, 21
　methods of use, 28
　reasons for using, 17, 20
　signs of abuse, 76-77
Southey, Robert, 7
Sudden Sniffing Death (SSD), 14, 41-42
suffocation, 18, 21, 41, 54

T
Tenenbein, Milton, 56
Texas Prevention Partnership, 88-89
tolerance, 25
toluene, 23-24, 31-33

U
University of Michigan, 17, 60, 63

V
volatile, 7, 16, 18, 20

W
Weiss, Harvey, 57, 89
Wells, Horace, 7, 11
Whippets™, 53
Wilmes, David. J., 64
withdrawal, 25

BMCNHS LIBRARY